THE MYSTERY AT MOLD MARKET

A NESTA GRIFFITHS MYSTERY

P. L. HANDLEY

CHAPTER 1

"That's two cups from the green bag for breakfast, two cups from the blue one around midday, two cups from the pink one for dinner — mam! Are you listening?"

Erin almost threw the metal bowl in her hand across the room and turned around to face her mother.

Nesta was staring at the enormous bags of dog food, but her gaze was distant, as though she had tuned out long ago. "Of course I'm listening."

"And you'll remember this for later?" Erin asked.

"I *do* own a dog," said Nesta. "You seem to forget that."

Her daughter cringed. "Yes, but Taylor and Kim need their routine. They won't eat it otherwise." She pointed towards the two cockapoos sitting in the corner of the kitchen, curiously watching them. Both were named after a pair of famous American women that Nesta had never heard of, and the two dogs seemed to possess a certain attitude that the retired teacher from Bala did not like one bit. The words "spoiled brats" sprang to mind, and the two well-groomed canines seemed to act as though they were the queens of the house.

"Dogs don't need a three-course meal," said Nesta, crossing her arms.

"But they do need *three* square meals," said Erin. She turned her lodger's attention to the pile of cans. "Now, once you've added the biscuits and poured the warm water — make sure it's not too hot, mind — then you need to add the dog meat."

"There's more?" Nesta clutched her own forehead and felt a migraine coming on.

"I haven't even gone through the snacks yet," said Erin with a shake of her hair (something which received as much attention as Taylor and Kim).

The salon owner had never been interested in having children, but when it came to her two cockapoos, she was as maternal as anything. Erin had been very relieved when her mother agreed to dogsit for two weeks, and now she was a barrel of nervous energy. Perhaps her holiday to Greece had been a bad idea after all, and she dreaded the thought of something going wrong whilst she was away.

"Will you relax?" asked Nesta. "This isn't fine dining we're talking about. You're not teaching me how to cook."

"Oh," said Erin. "That reminds me." She hurried over to the counter and picked up an envelope.

Nesta accepted the item with great trepidation. "What's this?"

Erin let out a beaming smile. "Open it and you'll find out. I had to get you something to say thank you."

Her mother sighed and shook her head. "You really didn't need to. I've got my stall, remember? You've saved me the commute."

"Just shut up and open it," said Erin.

Nesta ripped open the envelope and pulled out a card with a folded-up piece of paper inside. She unfolded the mysterious document to reveal a gift certificate with the words: *The Great*

Mold Bake Off. "A cookery class?" she asked with a raised eyebrow. "You've signed me up for a *cooking* class?"

"Not cooking," said Erin. "Baking!"

"Are you saying that I can't bake?" Nesta asked, trying to conceal her horror.

Her daughter placed a hand on her back. "Now, come on, mam. You've seen what your scones are like. They're like rocks."

"Do you realise how painful that is?"

"Yes," said Erin, clutching her stomach. "Very painful. I'm the one who had to eat them my entire childhood, remember? But that's not the point — you've always said you wanted a chance to flex your baking muscles."

"This is a *beginner* course," said Nesta, holding out the gift certificate like a dirty handkerchief.

"I'm sure you'll get to try some new things." Erin shot her arms up in the air. "It'll be fun!"

"And when am I going to find time to do this?" Nesta pointed to the pile of knitted items over on the table. "I've got my stall to prepare for."

Erin sighed. "The baking classes are in the evenings, mam. You'll have loads of time."

Her mother folded up her arms in a sulk. Nesta had booked her market stall slot months ago and was looking forward to finally getting the chance to sell her range of hand-knitted items. Her late husband had always admired her talent for knitting and had often encouraged her to make a side-business out of it. Now that she was retired, Nesta had decided that a market stall would be the perfect opportunity to top up her pension — and what better location than Mold Market?

Her daughter had lived in the Flintshire town for many years, and Nesta always enjoyed the excuse to visit (if not just for the impressive range of charity shops). Yr Wyddgrug (as it was called in Welsh) was only an hour's drive from her hometown of

Bala, but Mold was like a whole other world to this Gwynedd local. For one thing, the town had its very own *Home Bargains* — and a *McDonald's* (a restaurant that Nesta hadn't eaten in since the late nineties). Two weeks in Mold was like a city getaway, and Nesta was determined to savour every moment.

"So where exactly is this baking class?" Nesta asked.

"I think it's near the library," said Erin.

"Mold has a library?"

"Of course! Doesn't every town?"

Nesta began salivating at the thought of a whole new batch of murder mystery titles. She must have gone through the ones at her Bala library many times over.

"God, mam," Erin continued. "You really need to get out more. Take a few holidays. Go on a few coach trips or something. Isn't that what retired people are supposed to do?"

Her mother frowned. "Coach trips? How old do you think I am?"

"You know what I mean." Erin fetched a sheet of laminated paper from the kitchen counter and handed it to her new lodger.

"What's this?" Nesta asked.

"Your house itinerary." Erin turned her attention to the various columns and telephone numbers. "There's info about the boiler, fuse box and any contacts you might need if something goes wrong."

The older woman felt her jaw tighten and tried to look appreciative. "You really have thought of everything," she said. "I feel like I'm staying in a hotel."

"It's more like an *AirBnB*," said Erin, moving on with her tour.

"An Air — what?"

Before she could get an answer, her daughter was already going through the available food on offer, as if she would have starved to death otherwise.

"I've done my best to load up the fridge. But you'll need to keep an eye on the sell-by-dates."

"You mean," said Nesta, "I'll have to go out and look for milk? Heavens! How will I survive?"

Erin rolled her eyes. "Worst-case scenario," she said, "you've got my number. I've got plenty of roaming and data on my phone."

Nesta had no idea what her last sentence was referring to, and she was beginning to wonder whether her daughter had forgotten that the person standing in her kitchen had also given birth to her.

"I'll be fine," said Nesta. "We're in Mold, remember? It's hardly The Bronx. What could possibly go wrong in *this* town?"

CHAPTER 2

"Taylor! Kim! Stop that — right now!"

The two cockapoos took little notice of their new dog sitter and continued to bark at the weary Jack Russell hiding underneath the table. Hari growled at the pair of barking faces, as Nesta tried to get herself in between them.

"This is Hari's dinner time, too, you nasty little things. Let him eat with you in peace." Her words had fallen on deaf ears, and the two siblings stood their ground beside the bowls of food. Nesta sighed and turned to Hari. "It's alright," she said. "Let these two divas eat up, and I'll give you a little extra in the other room."

Now that Erin and her boyfriend had grabbed their suitcases and headed off for their Greek holiday, the house was all Nesta's (until she had realised who the *real* owners were).

"I know what we need," said Nesta, raising her arms up in the air. "A nice walk!"

Erin's front door was a lot harder to open than her own one back in Bala, and Nesta was forced to give it a hard nudge to escape. The townhouse was located on a quiet road at the top end of town and faced the edges of an enormous, walled mound called Bailey Hill. What had previously served as a Norman castle was now a popular site for dog walks and visitors, where a person could quite easily get lost along its narrow paths. The remains of an actual castle were long gone, but there were still a number of ancient ruins to be found if someone looked hard enough.

Nesta had barely made it to the bailey's main gate before she realised that a steep climb might not have been the best idea. Unlike Hari, who was well up for a hike, Taylor and Kim had already started pulling on their dog leads.

"Come along," she said to them. "It will be worth it when we get up there. Think of the exercise!"

The two cockapoos couldn't think of anything worse and wanted desperately to return to the sanctuary of their perfectly-heated home.

Once she had finally convinced them to follow her inside the stone walls, Nesta slammed the iron gate shut and took a deep breath. "There, that wasn't so bad, was it?"

Those two furry faces stared at her and sat themselves down in protest. Despite the dog leads stretching out between them all, they would not be going any further.

Hari was stood only a few feet away, watching, as he was curious to see what his owner intended to do next. It was clear that these two cockapoos were not budging.

"Fine," said Nesta, marching towards them. "If you don't like being on a lead, then let's try you without one."

The Jack Russell tilted his head, observing, as though he could sense what was about to happen next. Nesta unclipped the lead from each collar, and the moment she turned her back, Taylor and Kim made a quick dash up the hill. "Hey!" she cried.

The two canines took no notice and had soon disappeared through the nearest cluster of trees.

"Come back here!" Nesta cried. "Right now!"

What followed was a chase that lasted all of several minutes. The steep path played havoc with Nesta's tight calves, and she huffed and puffed her way to the nearest clearing, where a children's playpark was silent and empty.

"Taylor! Kim!"

The two dogs were nowhere to be seen, and Hari began circling the cute, wooden climbing frame in a giant loop. It was something he had done since he was a puppy, especially at the sight of an open space.

"Oh, for heaven's sake," Nesta muttered under her breath. "What have I done?"

She pressed forward and headed further into the bailey, calling out at regular intervals. A narrow path took her down a slope that seemed to go on forever, as she fought back the wild overgrowth that clawed at her from either side. For an area of land that was entirely walled off, the Bailey Hill had a tendency to make a person feel quite lost amongst its trees and bushes. Its narrow footpaths snaked around like a cruel maze, and Nesta was beginning to wonder whether it would ever end.

"Kim! Taylor!"

Her cries echoed into the air and were accompanied by chirping noises from up above. It was probably the vultures circling her, she thought. After almost tripping up on another hole, she was relieved to join a new footpath, one that appeared to follow the outer wall. Now she could find out exactly how large this ancient mound was and hopefully track down her stray dogs. Hari followed closely at her heels, his nose rummaging through the dirt like a hairy vacuum cleaner.

Just as Nesta was beginning to lose all hope, she heard a high-pitched yelp from up above, causing her to stop suddenly and look around. When it became apparent that the noise had come from higher ground, she made the steep climb to a levelled area with a circle of twelve standing stones. These carefully arranged stone structures reminded her of a horror film that she had once seen involving a disturbing pagan ritual. The flat-topped pillars were so distracting that she hadn't even noticed the figure standing in the middle.

"Oh," she said, turning to the mysterious gentleman in a tweed sporting jacket and flat cap. She was relieved to find him alone and not surrounded by a circle of druids.

"Are these yours?" asked the stranger. He pointed to the two cockapoos beside his feet.

Nesta almost had to do a double-take. Whoever those two dogs were, they certainly had not been the same ones she had entered the bailey with. Perhaps this man really *was* a druid after all.

"*There* you two are," she said, heading over to them with open arms. Taylor and Kim both let out a bark and disappeared behind the man's boots. Nesta paused and let out a frustrated *huff*. "Well, I don't know what sort of spell you've cast over them, but I'd like you to teach me it."

The man smirked. "I've owned a few dogs over the years," he said, reaching out his hand. "Charlie."

"So have I," said Nesta, who wanted to point out that these two cockapoos were a whole different kettle of fish. She shook his hand. "Nesta."

"All dogs have their quirks," said Charlie.

Nesta grabbed her pair of leads and began chasing the dogs around his legs. "If that's true, these two are very quirky indeed." She eventually gave up and threw her arms in the air.

"May I?" asked Charlie. He took the leads from her and effortlessly clipped them to the cockapoos.

Nesta wanted to put a lead on *him* and choke the smug man to death with it. "You can keep them if you like."

Charlie turned to her with a playful smile and whispered: "You want to know the secret?" He reached inside his jacket pocket and pulled out a *Peperami*. "They're an easy way to a dog's heart."

Nesta watched in disgust, as he fed one of his snacks to Taylor and Kim. "That's cheating."

"All is fair in love and war," said Charlie. "And I know all about that."

"Love?" asked Nesta. "Or war?"

The man in traditional hunting gear gave her questions some thought. "Both, actually."

"You served in the military?" Judging by the man's well-groomed appearance and formal attire, she would not have been surprised.

"Just a bit," said Charlie. "More than I've been in love, anyway."

They both turned to admire the circle of stones and shared a short silence.

"They're beautiful, aren't they?" Charlie asked.

"They're... something." Nesta scratched her head. "What are they doing in a spot like this? I never knew Mold had its own Stonehenge."

Charlie chuckled. "I wouldn't compare this to a prehistoric, megalithic structure like *Stonehenge*."

Nesta gave him a frosty glare. "That's quite a mouthful," she said. "I can see that you must spend a lot of your time around ancient stone monuments."

"This was laid out in the early nineteen-twenties," said Charlie, pointing to the formation.

"Oh," said Nesta with a blush. "Well, I suppose there's a slight gap between the two. How on earth do you know that?"

"It mentions it in the museum."

"Mold has a museum?"

"Above the library."

"Ah," said Nesta. "This library is the gift that keeps on giving. Is that why you're here, then? Seeing the sights?"

"Something like that." Charlie's face turned serious. "But I also live here. Mold's history has always held a special place in my heart."

Nesta nodded. "You don't sound very local. Where are you from?"

"Here, there and everywhere. I moved to Mold about ten years ago from Caernarfon."

"Ah," said Nesta, who was impressed with the man's proper pronunciation. "Now *there's* a castle."

Charlie nodded. "Although, the original Mold castle would likely pre-date that." His historical knowledge continued to impress the woman beside him, who, despite being an English teacher, was still partial to a spot of history herself.

They both turned around and looked up towards the great mound beside them, reaching up towards the sky.

"Have you been up to the top, yet?" Charlie asked.

Moments later, and the two explorers were making their way up a long flight of stone steps. Taylor and Kim reluctantly tagged along in the hope of another snack and Hari was already off in front.

"They could have made these steps a bit smaller," said Nesta, huffing and puffing her way up. "Those Normans weren't very practical."

Charlie, despite being older than the woman beside him, seemed to be coping a lot better with the climb, which only infuriated Nesta more. Damn that army background of his, she thought.

When they finally reached the top, Nesta could have easily begun leaping up and down like Rocky Balboa (had she possessed any energy left).

"What do you think?" asked Charlie.

Nesta had been too focused on her heart rate to even notice the impressive view, and she spun around to take it all in.

"I've never seen Mold from this angle before," she said.

Charlie nodded. "It's a great place to call home."

The woman beside him was busy squinting to see if she could spot *Theatr Clwyd*.

He turned to her with a smile. "I'm surprised that I haven't seen you around before."

Nesta saw his friendly gaze and realised that she hadn't mentioned her situation. "Oh, I'm not local, I'm afraid. I live in Bala."

"Bala?" The man struggled to hide his disappointment.

"Yes, I'm only here for two weeks. My daughter lives in town, and I'm looking after her two —" She had to stop herself from saying the word "*babies*".

Charlie looked down at the restless cockapoos and put two and two together. "Ah, that makes sense. Well, you're just in time for market day. Every Wednesday and Saturday."

Nesta's face lit up. "It's funny you should say that. I'm going to be running my very own stall."

"Is that right?" asked Charlie, slightly intrigued.

"I've always wanted to give it a go." Nesta rubbed her hands together, as she envisioned queues of people all lining up to buy her hand-knitted items. "And if there's one thing I'm learning in my retirement — it's never too late to try something new."

"I can't argue with that," said Charlie. "I'll be around town tomorrow. I'll have to come and have a browse. Maybe you can give me a discount."

Nesta smiled. "It depends. Do you like the idea of a knitted cardigan? Or how about a pair of mittens?"

"I'll wear anything at the right price."

They both turned to admire the panoramic view one last time. The rooftops of Mold glowed in the August evening sun, and Nesta could see the tower of St Mary's Church poking up in the distance.

Charlie bid his new friend a brief farewell once they had emerged from the walls of Bailey Hill. Little did Charlie know it, but the sunset he had just witnessed up on the mound was to be his last.

CHAPTER 3

When it came to Wednesday mornings, Mold High Street was very much an early bird. By six o'clock, the entire main road had been blocked off, and the market traders were already setting up their stalls. It was a weekly tradition that many of the regulars had grown accustomed to, as they popped up their tables and arranged their own unique goods.

There were all the usual suspects: baker Simon Rodgers and his son Jake; Sean Lyons and his butcher van; Wendy Stephens and her modest cake stall; Melanie and Evan with their fruit and veg stand; Samir Mandal with his large range of shoes; Millie Hogan and her niche selection of dream catchers and scented candles; Mark Hutson and his record selection; Oskar Pakulski with his popular burger van.

All the regulars were present that day, including a trader that many did not recognise. Nesta Griffiths was positioned in the side street leading to Daniel Owen Square. Named after a Welsh novelist from the nineteenth century, the square also hosted its fair share of market stalls.

Nesta was quite pleased with her designated spot and hoped

she could snag a good chunk of the passing traffic once the town had come to life.

Her range of knitted items were already laid out across her stall: hats, jumpers, mittens, stuffed toys — she had spent the best part of a year creating her precious stock and was beginning to feel quite reluctant to sell it now that the time had come. It had been almost impossible to work out a price for goods that had taken her more time to create than she would have liked to admit. If she had been paid by the hour for each knitted jumper, then the stall in front of her would have been worth a small fortune.

"What we got here, then?"

Nesta looked up to see a man with the largest hands she had ever seen. Sean Lyons was dressed in a white coat with a stripy red apron over the top. He stared down at her knitted goods, whilst puffing away on a cigarette.

"Do you see anything you like?" asked Nesta.

Sean let out a croaky chuckle. "I don't come here to buy." He offered out his hand. "I'm your new neighbour."

Nesta looked over at the meat van nearby and accepted the butcher's handshake.

Sean noticed her fascination with his hands and flicked out his fingers like a piano player. "You not seen a butcher's hands before?" he asked. "These are the result of handling freezing cold meat for thirty years."

"It must be tough during the winter months," said Nesta.

"Nah!" Sean shrugged off her concern and puffed out his chest. "I've killed off all the nerves, you see. Can't feel a thing with these hands anymore. You get used to the cold after a while. I learnt that pretty quickly as an apprentice. I've been doing this a long time."

"Any tips?" Nesta gave him an eager smile. "It's my first day."

Sean chuckled. "I've heard that before. This market life is

not for everybody. I've seen more people disappear than my reduced pork chops." He scratched his head and gave her question some thought. "Tips? Well... it's quite simple, really. There's two parts to making money in this game — find a product that people want to buy — supply and demand! That's one rule that never changes. Luckily for me, people always need to eat."

Nesta could see his cynical gaze, as he inspected one of her bobble hats. "Are you implying that my knitwear isn't going to sell?" she asked.

The butcher placed a hand on his chest and tried to act surprised. "I wouldn't dream of it!" He leant in and lowered his voice. "Just don't get your hopes up. It's a hard sell in summer."

Nesta glared at him with furious eyes. She couldn't wait to wipe that smug grin off his face. "Well, seeing as you're such an expert, what's the *second* part of your little sales philosophy?"

Sean stood tall like a caped superhero. "Salesmanship! You can have the best products in the world, but they're useless if you can't sell them. You got to work the crowd — make them come back next week."

"And is that what you do?" asked Nesta. "Work the crowd?"

"Oh, aye! My customers are very loyal. They don't just buy a fillet steak — they buy me!"

Nesta stared at the man. Had it been *her* buying Sean Lyons, she would have asked for a refund.

"Think about it," Sean continued. "If they didn't, then why not just buy their meat from the supermarket? The business isn't the meat — it's yours truly."

"Well," said Nesta, imagining herself roasting the butcher in an oven. "I appreciate your friendly advice. But I think I'll do just fine."

Sean chuckled. "That's the spirit." He lifted up one of the tiny cardigans. "And, hey — worst-case scenario — I'm sure you've got plenty of grandkids, right? They'll be happy to take all this off your hands."

He gave her a wink, before she snatched the cardigan out of his hands.

~

Darren Price had taken two buses to get to his final destination and had still only reached the outskirts of Mold. The teenager from Bala had struggled to pass the time during the school summer holidays and had been glad for the excuse to earn some extra money. Nesta had even offered to cover his bus fare but had conveniently forgotten to mention that he would take almost two hours to get there.

Darren and Nesta had formed an unlikely relationship since the murder of Dafydd Thomas, and they would hardly describe each other as friends. Neither one of them could think of a word to describe their strange association, but it seemed to come in useful from time to time. On this occasion, Nesta was able to acquire a spare pair of hands to handle the hoards of customers that were going to descend on her little knitting stall, and Darren had an opportunity to make an extra forty pounds to buy those pair of trainers he'd been keen on.

By the time he had arrived on Mold high street, the market was already buzzing with people, and he became distracted by a stall selling t-shirts with popular band names across the front. Perhaps, he thought, his new employer could throw in an Iron Maiden t-shirt as a bonus payment.

When he finally reached the stall of knitwear down the narrow side street, a furious Nesta was ready to clobber him.

"What time do you call this?" she asked. "You know I'm paying you by the hour?"

An innocent Darren waved out his arms. "I've been sat on a

bus for two hours!" He glanced down at the hand-knitted items. "Is this really what we're selling?"

The woman behind her stall frowned. "We won't be with an attitude like *that*. It's all about working the crowd."

Darren joined her behind the table and shook his head. "Nobody's going to buy this sort of stuff in summer."

Nesta forced out her words through gritted teeth. "You can sell anything if you put your mind to it."

"*Almost* anything," said Darren, lifting up a pair of mittens.

Before Nesta was tempted to start knitting her very own noose, she grabbed her handbag. "Fancy a coffee? I'd better grab them before the rush starts."

"You can probably take your time," said Darren. He saw her furious expression and decided to smile. "Hot chocolate, please."

Nesta headed in the direction of the high street through a stream of busy shoppers. Even on a Wednesday, Mold market was crowded with visitors from all over the county, many of them having traveled specially for a chance to peruse the wide range of offerings on display.

The temptation to shop was too much even for Nesta, who always found it hard to resist a good bargain. If she was not careful, this first-time trader could have ended up spending more than she was making, especially when it came to the stall full of cakes.

"Two for a pound!" the woman behind her cupcake stand shouted.

Further along was a stall full of antiques, consisting of several trinkets that Nesta tried to picture above her fireplace. "Stop it," she muttered to herself, quickly shaking her burning desires away. "Focus on the task in hand."

The appearance of a pop-up coffee stand gave the woman a moment of relief. She approached a young woman with bright purple hair knocking up her beautifully-crafted lattes in the back of a trailer. Nesta stared at the image of a swan in one of the milky foams and felt saddened at the fact that someone was about to drink it.

"These look wonderful," she said, causing the young woman to look up and smile.

"Thanks," said Claire, wiping the chocolate powder off her hands. "What can I get you?"

"A hot chocolate and a coffee, please."

Claire smiled. "We've got flat whites, cappuccinos, frappuccinos, mochas, macchiatos..."

Nesta took an enormous gulp. "I'll have one of those swans, please."

The young woman nodded and began firing up her machine with the precision of a trained professional. Nesta watched with great fascination, until her attention was distracted by a familiar figure over in the distance.

"Is everything alright?" asked Claire, handing over the finished latte. She saw her customer staring in the direction of a stall selling army surplus clothing and a range of camping equipment. Behind the counter was Charlie Coogan, the man from the bailey.

"Uh, yes," said Nesta, taking hold of her coffee. "I just spotted someone I know."

Claire scrunched up her nose as though she was inhaling a blocked drain. "Charlie? He's a friend of yours?"

"Oh, no." Nesta took a sip of her coffee and stared at the man dressed in his old uniform. "We only met yesterday. But he seemed like a nice enough chap."

The young barista scoffed. "Yeah, right. Nice enough to make money out of selling dead animals, you mean?"

"Excuse me?"

"The guy's got a load of taxidermy on sale." Clarie pointed

towards Charlie's stall. Nesta squinted and could just about make out some furry objects sitting on the counter.

"Oh, I see. So he has. I'm sure he didn't actually kill the animals himself, though." She turned to see the young woman's raised eyebrow. "Now, come on. Surely not."

"Mr Action Man over there?" Claire asked. "You think a bloke that sells army-themed clothes and equipment doesn't own a few guns at home?"

Nesta shook her head. "You have a very vivid imagination, young lady."

Claire shrugged. "I just say what I see. And I see a warmongering maniac who likes to shoot things. I'm not the only one who doesn't like him. He's got quite the reputation around here."

"What sort of reputation?" Nesta didn't get a response and was handed her spare change. After another gulp of coffee, she saw Charlie waving at her.

"We meet again," the man said, as she approached his stall.

"We do indeed," said Nesta, giving him a disapproving frown. "You didn't tell me you worked at the market."

Charlie gave her an innocent smile. "I thought I'd surprise you."

Nesta gazed down at the row of Swiss Army knives and compasses. Fortunately, she thought, there was no firearm in sight. "Consider me very surprised." She did her best to avoid eye contact with the taxidermy. "Do you hunt?"

Now it was Charlie's turn to be surprised. "Whatever gave you that idea?" He gave her a playful smile that was not reciprocated. "I don't kill for sport, if that's what you mean. Anything I've ever hunted, I've taken home and eaten. Fish, game, deer — even rabbits!"

"I haven't come here to judge," said Nesta. "I was raised on a farm." She looked down at the stuffed weasel. "I'm just not a fan of hunting, that's all. It makes me a little uncomfortable."

"Fair enough." Charlie nodded. "Just because I kill doesn't mean I don't respect life, you know? We're all animals at heart."

"Some more than others."

The man behind his stall laughed. "How's your first day on the market going?"

Nesta looked down at her coffee and felt a sudden tingle of guilt. She hoped Darren was coping alright. "It's early days. How long have you been doing this for?"

"In Mold? A few years. But I've been working on market stalls since I was a young lad. My old man used to work at Covent Garden. It's all I've ever done outside of the military."

"Is that where you're from?" Nesta asked. It explained his accent, she thought. "London?"

"I'm from a lot of places," said Charlie. "I moved around a lot when I was younger."

"What sort of things did your father sell?"

"Everything!" Charlie laughed. "He was a real Del Boy Trotter. Always full of ideas. He loved the markets. There's something really pure about it. Anyone can sell anything you like. And if you can make the goods yourself — even better. There's a reason people still flock to the market. Online shopping doesn't hold a candle to a face-to-face purchase."

Nesta nodded. "You'd get on quite well with a butcher I know." She turned around and looked up at the clock on St Mary's Church. "Heavens! I should get going."

Charlie saluted her. "Good luck! Oh, and if you see an elderly woman called Dorothy — don't let her waste your time. She's an absolute nightmare. Ask anyone. She never buys anything!"

His cries of warning followed Nesta all the way back to her stall. As she had decided earlier, Nesta didn't need any advice or help. She could cope perfectly fine on her own.

"Where did you get that coffee?" Darren asked upon her return. "Costa Rica?"

"Don't *you* start talking about being late," Nesta snapped. She handed him his hot chocolate and inspected her layout. It hadn't changed very much. "How are we doing? What's the takings?"

Darren stared at her. "You mean, how much have we made?" He opened up the ice cream container on the table and pulled out a twenty pence coin. "That couple selling fruit and veg asked for one of our boxes. So I said they had to pay for it." He pointed to the side of his head. "Them are proper business skills."

Nesta sighed. "Yes, well done, Alan Sugar. Maybe we should just sell cardboard boxes."

"Not a bad idea!"

"I was joking."

"Oh."

They both turned to see a woman approaching. Nesta leant across to whisper in her assistant's ear: "Here comes one. She's looking at our stall."

"Just play it cool," Darren whispered back. "Or you'll scare her off."

"Are these hand-knitted?" asked the curious woman. She hunched over with her terrible posture and pointed her cane at the items in front of her.

"Every single one," said Nesta with a proud smile.

The woman let out a grunt. "What's that supposed to be?" She pointed at one of the stuffed toys which sat there begging to be purchased.

"It's a penguin, madam."

"Hmh," the customer muttered. "Strangest penguin I've ever seen."

Darren let out a snort of laughter and was nudged by his business partner.

"What are those things?" She pointed to a small pile of festive-themed objects.

"Ah," said Nesta, leaping over to lift up a knitted Robin with a loop on his head. "I see you have splendid taste. These are our range of Christmas tree decorations."

The confused woman stared at her. "Christmas? It's August."

Nesta coughed. "Yes, well — a lot of people like to buy their Christmas decorations all year round."

The woman looked up at the passing rows of shoppers. "Do they?"

"Yes," Nesta said firmly through gritted teeth. She was beginning to lose her patience already and took a deep breath. The customer was not always right, she realised. "How about some of our hats?" She popped on one of her bobble hats and did a little catwalk. "I'm Nesta, by the way. Always nice to meet a local."

The two shook hands.

"Dorothy," said the elderly woman.

Nesta's heart sank, as Charlie's words of warning echoed in her ears. She took a deep sigh and turned to an oblivious Darren. "Another hot chocolate?"

CHAPTER 4

Once Nesta had returned to her stall with another round of drinks, she was ready to do business. Unfortunately for her, business continued to be slow (and the word *slow* on *this* market stall actually meant no business at all). Crowds of people flowed past without giving her business the slightest bit of attention, and she began to wonder whether the whole venture had been a stupid idea in the first place.

Every now and again, she turned to glance over at Sean Lyons' meat truck and could hear the butcher's loud cries echoing away down the alleyway.

"Get your chops! Three for a fiver! Go on — treat yourself for dinner! What about you, sir? You could do with a bit of meat on you!" His cheerful gaze landed on Nesta's stare. "Or you, madam?! Over by the woolly jumpers! One of these spicy steaks should warm you up!"

His loud cackle made her cringe. "I'll show him," she muttered under her breath.

"What was that?" asked Darren, who was sitting on a plastic crate reading a magazine.

"Will you try and look enthusiastic about what we're doing?" Nesta asked. The confused young man gave her a blank stare. "How are we supposed to excite our customers if we can't excite ourselves?"

"Excited?" Darren pointed at the range of knitted items. "About *them*?"

Nesta shook her head. "This isn't working. We have to do something..." She turned to the passersby and cupped her mouth. "Roll up! Roll up! Get your knitted mittens! Two for a pound!"

The passing faces simply stared at her as though she had gone senile (and she was beginning to wonder if in fact she had).

Darren placed a hand on her shoulder. "I don't think that's working."

"I *know* it's not working," Nesta snapped before regretting her outburst. "I'm sorry. I just didn't think it would be this hard."

The teenager felt a sudden flutter of pity and tried to rack his brains for an idea. "What if I go around the market wearing some of your knitted accessories? You know, make it fashionable. I could go undercover."

Nesta turned to him and smiled. She could see the genuine enthusiasm in his face. "That's very sweet of you. But nobody around here's going to think you're fashionable."

The teenager folded up his arms and frowned. "What's that supposed to mean?"

As she tried to think of a response that would avoid causing any further offence, Nesta noticed a young couple in the background behind him, admiring someone's beautiful labrador. "I've got an idea."

"An idea for what?" asked Darren, as he watched her grabbing her handbag.

"Hold the fort for me, would you?" She began walking in the

direction of the high street. "I'll be back in ten. I just need to check on the dogs."

Darren flung his arms in the air, helplessly, and returned to his magazine. "I should have got a job at the Co-op."

Nesta marched through the busy street, until she crossed over and left the market behind. The road leading back past St Mary's Church was much quieter, and it was hard not to admire the building's impressive exterior. The fifteenth-century structure had always been a dominating fixture in this small town with its tower of powerful bells and Gothic architecture. It was hard to ignore and could be seen from most areas of Mold.

She continued on, away from the hustle and bustle, until she reached her daughter's front door opposite Bailey Hill.

Her entrance into the house was accompanied by a series of excited barks from Hari and the two cockapoos. Nesta's face fell at the sight of Erin's prized sofa which had now been torn to shreds by a pair of toothy snouts. Come to think of it, Erin *had* told her mother not to leave them alone in the living room and to keep the kitchen door closed when leaving the house (a detail that Nesta had chosen to ignore).

Hari sat in the corner of the room looking smug, having witnessed this pair of mischievous cockapoos unleash their destruction. He knew there would be trouble when his owner got home, and here she was.

"Oh, Taylor… Kim… what have you done?"

∼

Nesta's return journey to the market was not an easy one. Now she had three dogs on a lead with two of them tugging her all over the pavement.

"Now, stop that! Taylor, Kim — there's no need to pull."

Even Hari was finding it difficult being yanked from side to side, as his owner struggled to maintain a straight line. Once he had pulled the cockapoos back in the opposite direction, Nesta had no chance of maintaining order and was like a heron on a jet ski. It was quite surprising how much force three small dogs could achieve with the right kind of determination, and she couldn't believe what time it was when the hourly church bell rang up ahead.

"Right," Nesta snapped. "That's enough! We need to get back to the stall."

The sound of an amused giggle made her look up towards a nearby bench overlooking the main road.

"Are they taking you for a walk?" asked the woman on the bench.

The sight of an entertained Dorothy made Nesta's heart sink, and she was about to shout out in protest, when she heard a loud gunshot.

All three of her dogs began barking, and she froze on the spot.

"Did you hear that?" asked Nesta.

"Hear what?" asked Dorothy.

Nesta pointed in the direction of the church. "That loud *bang*! It sounded like a gun."

The elderly woman jiggled her own ear. "I've not got my hearing aids in," she said. "You'll have to speak up."

"Never mind," Nesta muttered and made a dash for the church.

Her three dogs were no longer fighting against her and followed alongside, as they hurried up the stone steps. The front doors were open when she approached the entrance, and a vicar came running outside in a flustered state.

"Did you hear that?" Nesta asked.

The Reverend Colin Johnson nodded and pointed to the

back of the church. "It came from that direction." He began leading the way around the side of the building.

Nesta and her dogs followed him across the freshly-cut grass.

They headed past several lines of gravestones, until a figure up ahead caused them both to stop. The person up in the distance was lying flat on his back beside one the graves, and it didn't take a forensic expert to work out that he had been shot in the chest.

Nesta recognised the face immediately, and she had to pull her barking dogs away. The vicar beside her was visibly shocked, and they were soon joined by a third witness in a hi-vis jacket.

Groundskeeper Jason Potts had abandoned his lawnmower on the other side of the church and let out a gasp of his own when he saw the body. "I know that man!" he cried. "He has a stall over at the market."

Nesta nodded. "His name's Charlie Coogan."

CHAPTER 5

"He's been *shot*?"

Nesta hushed the excited teenager and smiled at a passing shopper. "Don't say it too loud. The public doesn't know yet."

Darren looked around with a cynical frown. "I wouldn't worry about people paying attention to *this* stall." The young man was struck by a bobble hat against his forehead and was glad she hadn't used the pair of knitting needles. "How do I always miss all the action?"

"I can assure you," said Nesta. "There was no action."

"Then how do you know he was shot?" asked Darren.

"I heard the gunshot. And I saw the aftermath."

Nesta had been keen to leave the scene of the crime as soon as possible. The last thing she wanted was for the sight of another dead body to haunt her dreams again, but it was too late for that. Fortunately, Mold had a sizable police station, and it hadn't taken long for the authorities to seal off the area and confirm their witnesses.

Still, Nesta had been forced to wait a few hours before she

was free to return to her stall, and her cover had been close to filing a missing person's report.

"What was he doing in a graveyard?" asked Darren.

"Who knows," said Nesta. "But I think the most important question is — why would someone want to shoot him? It was clearly premeditated. Nobody walks around with a rifle."

"How do you know it was a rifle?"

"My father used to own one back on the farm. I used to hear him shooting rats out in the sheds. Besides, it's a lot more likely than a handgun."

Darren was struggling to contain his excitement. Focusing on knitted goods suddenly felt even more boring than it had done *before* the shooting. Now, there was a killer on the loose, and he couldn't have been more ready. Wait until his *YouTube* subscribers heard about *this* one, he thought.

"What are you doing?" Nesta asked, as she turned to see him sticking his phone in her face. "Get that thing away from me! Are you trying to fry my brain with radiation waves?"

"It's fresh content for the channel," said Darren, hovering around her like a news camera operator. "We can get an eye-witness report. Live from Mold!"

Nesta rolled her eyes. She had heard enough about Darren's so-called true crime channel. The nature of an internet streaming channel still baffled her, and why anyone would want to tune in to such a thing was a bigger mystery than the murder of Charlie Coogan. According to Darren, his followers had trebled since his videos on the murder of Dafydd Thomas back in Bala, and the views on these videos had grown even more. Unfortunately, it wasn't easy running a true crime channel in a town where the crimes were few and far between and the content had taken a big dip in the months since. Apart from his video on the rumoured sheep rustling near Rhiwlas, he hadn't been able to post anything new at all.

"I didn't actually witness the murder itself," Nesta pointed out. "I found the body. Which is a habit I need to stop."

"That's good enough for me," said Darren. "And good enough for the viewers. How about you start with describing the body — the gorier, the better!"

"I will not be your little internet puppet," Nesta snapped. "You know my stance on the strange people who watch this nonsense. They're probably sitting there in their underwear — or worse!"

"They're probably the same kind of people who read your precious murder mystery books," said Darren. "It's all the same thing."

"Nonsense!" Nesta quickly tidied up her hair in case he was filming. "I honestly don't know why you waste your time with these videos."

"The money helps."

Nesta's eyes widened. The teenager's unexpected comment caused her to go silent for a moment.

"*What* money?"

Darren smiled. "The subs money." The woman in front of him stared in a manner that implied he would need to elaborate. "The more people you have that subscribe to your channel, the more you get paid."

"What's the limit?"

"There is no limit."

Nesta took a moment to let this sink in. "How many subscribers do you have?"

"A few hundred," said Darren. "Most of those were from the Dafydd Thomas videos. True crime audiences love a good murder mystery." The teenager could see a glimmer of intrigue in her eyes, like pound signs, and decided to put his new business hat on. "So how about it? If you help me get more content,

I'll give you twenty-five percent of everything the channel makes."

Nesta gave his offer some thought. As a person on a pension, any opportunity of a top-up was most welcome. "Fifty percent."

Darren gave her a disgusted frown. This retired teacher was as bad as the man who had tried to haggle them for a pair of knitted socks.

Seconds later, and Nesta was ready for her close-up, as she divulged the details into Darren's tiny phone lens. In some ways, she rather enjoyed the opportunity of documenting her thoughts in this brief video diary entry. She had kept a physical journal for most of her life and had stopped when her husband, Morgan, had died. She wasn't quite sure why she had stopped writing but certainly missed the therapeutic process of unloading her mind.

Once Darren had finished his video, his mind was racing at the thought of finding more content. "You said the guy's stall was on the high street?" he asked.

Nesta nodded. "He was a former member of the Welsh Guards. He sold military-themed goods and outdoor equipment."

Darren's eyes lit up. "Maybe he was shot by an enemy assassin!"

Nesta raised an eyebrow. "What enemy? We're not at war. And he was long retired from the military."

"Maybe it was revenge from the past. The assassin could have been in the church tower with a sniper rifle."

"Maybe you need to stop playing those dreadful video games." Nesta watched him head around the stall. "Where are you going?"

"To get some footage of the stall," said Darren, waving his camera. "There might be some clues."

"You can't just —" Before she could protest, Anita from the stall beside them was running past.

"They're closing the market," Anita cried.

"They're what?" asked Nesta.

"The police are cordoning off the whole road because of the shooting. The traffic will be a nightmare."

A disappointed Nesta turned to Darren. "I didn't even get a chance to try my idea."

"What idea?"

"My new strategy to get us more customers." Nesta looked down at her three dogs and then over at the pile of knitted dog clothes. "We'd have made a fortune."

Darren couldn't help but pity the woman and her so-called cunning plan. Unless her idea was to give away free alcoholic drinks with each purchase, he couldn't imagine It ever working.

"When's the next market day?" he asked.

"Saturday," said Nesta.

"I guess we'll have to try it then," Darren said, causing her mood to lift. The teenager couldn't wait to return to the scene of the crime and fill his boots with more videos. "Same time, same place?"

CHAPTER 6

It had been more than twenty-four hours since the death of Charlie Coogan, and the sun was already beginning to set on the town of Mold. Nesta sat on the warm decking in her daughter's back garden, whilst two cockapoos and a Jack Russell munched away from their dog bowls. She could see the clock tower of St Mary's Church, which had a distinct presence even from this distance.

Her Thursday had been rather uneventful, especially when compared with the events of the day before. She had taken Taylor and Kim on the longest walk of their lives, and everyone was exhausted. They had covered most of Mold over the course of their ambitious hike, including a small diversion to the Glasfryn, a gastropub located on the outskirts of the town. Sitting on the Glasfryn's outdoor table, Nesta was treated to a magnificent view of the green fields and rolling hills.

In a town that boasted a thriving nightlife and trendy shops, it was easy to forget that Mold was also surrounded by miles of beautiful countryside. The Clwydian Range was but a stone throw away, where the Moel Famau hill stood tall as the highest point in the county of Flintshire.

Hari, Taylor and Kim were fast asleep when Nesta left the house, and she made the short walk to Daniel Owen square. Without the hustle and bustle of the weekly market, the town appeared almost unrecognisable at this time of day, and she barely bumped into a single person on her way through narrow side streets.

She entered the square to the sound of a distant singing lesson taking place in one of the second floor buildings, and the young woman's voice echoed over her with an eerie melody. Following the directions on her gift certificate, Nesta headed down another side street and turned a sharp corner. A back door with a sign awaited her, and it read: *The Great Mold Bake Off - Upstairs*.

This mysterious entrance, far away from the beaten path, was a stark contrast to the bright and colourful flyer she had been given by her daughter, and Nesta had a sudden urge to turn back around. There was no smell of baking, and the lighting was dark and dingy. In the end, she continued on regardless.

When she reached the top of the stairs, a woman was standing there to greet her.

"Nesta Griffiths?"

It was too late to turn back now, Nesta thought.

"Excellent! We've been expecting you!"

"Wait," said Nesta, squinting at her face. "I know you — you're the woman with that cake stall on the market."

Wendy Stephens let out a grin that showed off her recently whitened teeth. She had more colours on her dress than a bag of *Liquorice Allsorts* and lipstick that would have made Elizabeth Taylor jealous.

"It's a small world in Mold," she said. "Always glad to meet a satisfied customer."

Nesta tried not to get hypnotised by her enormous earrings.

"Uh, no. Actually, I run a market stall as well. The one with all the knitting?"

Wendy twisted her red lips and shook her head. "Can't say I've noticed it."

"You're not the only one," Nesta muttered.

"Come," said Wendy, leading her down the hallway. "I'll introduce you to the rest of the class. Everyone's already here."

A tingle of nerves spread through Nesta's stomach, as she envisioned walking into a room full of judgemental students, all eager to begin. What she found instead was a converted office with three individuals placed behind their tables.

"Oh," she said. "Did you say *everyone*?"

"Nesta," said Wendy, "this is Mark, Joan and Rupert. Your fellow alumni." She rubbed her hands together with a giddy chuckle. The woman had always wanted to teach a class but had never quite found the right subject. She didn't possess much interest in education and had never pursued any higher education after school, but she *did* like the idea of an entire room hanging on her every word.

Wendy remembered watching her secondary school teachers in awe: the power, the control, the respect. Finally, she now had the opportunity to be a qualified instructor (even though her baking skills were technically self-taught). Wendy had planned this course for months, and now her bake-off could finally begin. She could be just like her idol and favourite reality TV judge, Paul Hollywood, who had his very own framed photograph up in her house. Simon Cowell could never hold a candle to Paul Hollywood and certainly didn't know his way around a nice Lemon Drizzle cake.

The trio of students all nodded at their late classmate, as Rupert checked his watch.

"I've seen you before, too," said Nesta, pointing at the man with gelled hair and an upright collar. He reminded her of a middle-aged Roger Daltery. "You're the man with that record stall."

Mark gave her a wink. "That's me. Never forget a pretty face, eh?"

"You're very observant," said Wendy, as she led Nesta to her table. "That should come in useful when following my baking instructions."

Nesta shuddered. She hated the thought of following a recipe and much preferred to go with her instincts. Preparing food, in her opinion, was not a science but an act of art and expression. Her daughter may not have appreciated it, but a lot of care and love had gone into her scones.

"Now don't be nervous," said Wendy, giving her a welcome pack. "Everyone's a beginner here. We're going to take things slow."

"Oh," said Nesta, "I'm not actually a beginner. I've been baking for most of my life."

Wendy placed a hand on her shoulder and gave the new student a patronising smile. "Ah, that's the spirit. In many ways, we all possess the ability to bake. I'm here to unlock it for you."

Nesta folded up her arms in a sulk and sat down behind her desk.

Wendy headed to the front of the class like a guest speaker at a *Ted Talk*. She had finally arrived in her rightful place.

"Hello, bakers." Uttering those words gave her a pleasure unlike anything she had experienced before. "Welcome. I'm here to take you on a journey of self-discovery. Baking is not just flour and butter — but a way of life. And I'm honoured to be the one to open your minds this week." She saw Rupert raising up his hand. "Uh, yes, Rupert."

The red-faced man with a crumpled shirt and hair that was balding from too much stress cleared his throat. "Will we be doing Battenberg cake?"

Wendy laughed. "Oh, that's very sweet. But we need to learn to crawl before we can walk."

"Don't you mean walk before you can run?" asked Nesta with a frown.

Wendy shook her head. "We are all but infants in this course. And there's no shame in that. Age is but a number when it comes to baking." She turned back to Rupert, who was disappointed by his answer. "You're not ready for a Battenberg just yet, dear. That will come on my advanced course — which is available for booking now, by the way. The info is in your welcome packs." The instructor clapped her hands. "Now, shall we begin?"

AFTER LAUNCHING into her demonstration of how to prepare a Victoria sponge cake, Wendy handed over the reins to her three students. Each one had been given their own mixing bowl, along with the standard ingredients and utensils.

"Remember," she said, "you need to put your soul into that mixture. A good cake is all in the prep. Don't rush it."

Her pupil, Joan, who had spent her teacher's entire lecture scribbling down notes, was frantically adding her ingredients, having dropped two eggs in the process. The nervous woman was putting far more than her soul into this cake, as the beads of sweat across her face dripped down at regular intervals. This moment was no different to her first day on the job as a dental assistant, where she had dropped countless cups of mouthwash over her patients. Nerves had always got the better of her, and she had hoped that a baking class might calm her down in the evenings.

"Deep breaths, Joan." Wendy marched back and forth in front of her table. "This is not a competition, remember?"

Someone who certainly *did* see it as a competition was Mark, who had already declared that he had finished and was propping up his feet on the table whilst humming out a tune.

Rupert was busy cursing into his bowl after adding a pair of glasses to the mixture and had already experienced trouble reading Wendy's instructions.

Nesta's instructions, on the other hand, were scrunched up into a ball at the corner of her table, and she continued to top-up her mixture as needed.

Once everyone had finished their first stage of the process, Wendy wheeled out her portable ovens, and it was time for the *real* baking to begin.

The four students were soon standing around, waiting for their sponges to rise behind their glowing windows.

Rupert and Joan were checking their bakes at regular intervals, whilst Mark and Nesta stood further back, trying to play it cool. Wendy had temporarily left the room, giving her students a moment to breathe.

"So what inspired you to take this course?" Nesta asked.

Mark chomped away on his chewing gum, which seemed to have lasted the entire evening. "Just helping out a mate," he said. "We go way back, me and Wendy. Thought I'd come for support."

Nesta suddenly became cautious and could no longer speak freely about what she *really* thought of her teacher. "That's very nice of you."

Mark shrugged. "Yeah, well. She's a good teacher. I respect passion. That's probably the musician in me."

The retired teacher beside him could agree on the "passion" part but was not so sure about her teaching. So far, the only thing she had learnt about baking was how complicated it could all be. Up until that day, she had never used a measuring cup — let alone a pair of scales. "Just scoop up the butter and stick it in" was her philosophy on the matter. She didn't need a calculator.

"You're a musician?" she asked, eventually (and not all that surprised).

"Oh, aye." Mark performed a little air guitar for her. "I've rocked The Shire loads of times."

"Flintshire?" asked Nesta.

"And Denbighshire," Mark added with a smug grin. "I got a band called The Gaggles. But I do a lot of solo work, too, nowadays. I played The Fat Boar only the other week. They call me Gooseman — record trader by day — rocker by night."

Nesta followed his chuckle with a polite laugh. "I can only imagine. Have you been working on the market long?"

"Decades," said Mark. "I've been selling records way before it was trendy again. People laughed at me for years. Records have stood the test of time: tapes, CDs, *Spotify*... then, all of a sudden, records are cool again. People aren't laughing now."

"My husband used to love his record player," said Nesta. "I used to hate dusting the flaming thing. I'm still waiting for landline telephones to come back into fashion."

Mark laughed. "Yeah, good luck with that. Those things have bitten the dust already."

His choice of words reminded Nesta of a certain incident. "It was quite a shock, yesterday, don't you think? That poor man."

"Who, Charlie?" Mark struggled to hide his disdain. "Can't say him and me ever really got on."

"You knew him?"

"We've worked a lot of the same markets over the years. Not just Mold. A lot of the regulars go all over. Charlie was the same. But we were like chalk and cheese. You wouldn't catch a bloke like me in the army." Mark stood up straight and performed a salute. "Yes, sir, no, sir — nah, you can forget all that. I'm a free spirit. He used to tell me to get a haircut." He paused to entertain an idea and smiled. "It's quite funny, really. A man like him goes to war for a living, and then ends up getting himself shot in a Welsh market town. Life's funny sometimes."

"Funny's one word for it," said Nesta.

"I think the bloke was struggling lately," Mark added.

"In what way?"

"Well, businesswise. He wasn't selling as much as he used to. I mean, I can understand why. All that army surplus stuff — who wants to buy that these days? I never saw anyone buying anything. His stall was always deserted."

Nesta sighed. "I know the feeling. It's not as easy as it looks."

"Sometimes I wondered if that stall was just some sort of front for something else."

"You think he was involved in criminal activity?"

Mark turned to her with a smirk. "You saw what happened to him. People don't get blown away for nothing."

The sound of that gunshot echoed in Nesta's mind again. Charlie had never struck her as a gangster — not that she had ever met one. The only gangsters she could picture were ones in nice hats who drove around during the American prohibition. Her father used to love watching films about those people.

Mark checked his watch. "Time's up," he said, scurrying off to his oven. He pulled out his tray of sponge and admired its golden surface. "Perfect."

Joan was glaring through her own oven window with a concerned face. "Mine just isn't rising properly."

"Give it time," said Nesta, placing her hand on the woman's shoulder. "It'll be fine."

"How is everyone doing?" asked Wendy, who returned into the room with an excited smile. She saw Mark's tray and rushed over. "Oh! That's beautiful, babe. Well done you!"

"How is mine burnt?" asked Rupert, lifting up an over-baked piece of sponge. "The instructions clearly said a hundred and eighty degrees! This oven needs testing!" He flung his tray down on the table and looked as though he were about to massacre the entire thing with a wooden spoon.

Wendy shook her head and tutted at him, before she wandered over to Nesta and Joan. "Oh, dear, dear." She pointed to the pair of gloopy-looking cakes. "I see we have soggy bottoms all round over here. Better luck next time."

The pair of deflated students were forced to look on, as Wendy strolled over to her so-called "bestie", Mark, and clapped her hands.

"Now we're talking," she announced. "Looks like we've found our new star baker!"

Mark performed a little bow and gladly shook her hand.

The sight of them both made Nesta want to vomit, and she turned to a disheartened Joan.

"Pay no attention," Nesta whispered. "You're doing great." She watched Wendy and Mark hugging each other. "If anyone's got soggy bottoms, it's those two."

CHAPTER 7

Saturday morning rolled around fairly quickly, and Nesta was up bright and early for her second day on the market. When she arrived in the high street, most of the other traders had barely finished putting up their steel frames. These veterans of the market assembled their stalls with effortless movements, having done the same routine for many years. Nesta found the whole scene quite fascinating and enjoyed soaking up the busy atmosphere, as people rushed around at a frantic pace. There was a feeling of excitement in the air, a sense of opportunity for the day ahead. There was money to be made, and every market trader wanted their piece.

Nesta imagined that a place like Wall Street or Canary Wharf had a similar environment at the start of a busy day, and these people were no different.

"You look keen," said a voice from nearby.

Nesta turned around to find Dorothy sitting on the bench beside her stall. She secretly wanted to hurry the woman along in case her presence was a curse but had no choice but to grin and bear it. "Fancy seeing you here, Dorothy."

"Yes," said the older woman. "I'm never too far away in this town. You could say that I'm something of a people-watcher."

Nesta could think of a few other terms to describe her, such as "busy-body" or "nosey parker". Each town seemed to have one of these and Mold was no different.

"Do you ever go home, Dorothy?"

The woman on the bench cackled. "This town *is* my home. I've been here all my life. I know everyone."

"But surely you have a house," said Nesta.

"Oh, yes. I have a bungalow just around the corner. But I'm a creature of habit, you see." Dorothy pointed down to her seat. "I'll be on this bench for another five minutes, then I'll go get my scratch cards. Then I have a little sit on the bench down near the library. Then the church. I'll be home in time for Corrie, mind."

It sounded exhausting, Nesta thought. "You must see a lot."

"Oh, aye." Dorothy chuckled. "I see everything from my benches." She gave a passing man a wave. "Alright, Tony!"

Nesta watched the exchange with great fascination. She knew what it was like to be a local in a small town, but this woman was on another level. It was almost as though she was part of the street itself.

"He runs the flower stall, doesn't he?" she asked.

Dorothy paused. "Who?"

"The man you just said hello to."

"What man?"

"Tony..."

"Tony?" Dorothy tried to think. "Oh! Yes, Tony! He's a nice man. Runs a flower shop, you know?"

"Does he, really?"

Nesta checked her watch and hoped that her teenage assistant would arrive soon.

"Yes, I've always liked Tony. Haven't seen him in yonks, mind. Ex-army, too."

"Tony?" asked Nesta. Her ears had suddenly pricked up.

"Where?" asked Dorothy. "Is he here today?" Before the other woman could respond, she checked her watch. "Blimey! Is that the time?" She lifted up her cane and hauled herself up from the bench. "I need to go get my —"

"Scratch cards?"

Dorothy grinned at her. "Yes! How did you know that?"

Nesta gave her a wink. "Lucky guess."

∽

Tony Cockle placed the last of his carnations down and stood back to admire the view. Setting up his flower stall had become a ritual that he took very seriously. He was almost religious about it, and everything had to be absolutely perfect.

Unlike many of the other displays on that street, his market stall was a living, breathing organism and required the utmost respect.

"Those chrysanthemums look nice."

Tony turned around to find Nesta admiring his work, and she was genuinely impressed. "I should have chosen flowers to sell. Although, they're probably not great for my hay fever."

The florist frowned. "It's not as easy as it looks. When it comes to flowers, they take a lot of planning. Nothing good lasts forever."

Nesta nodded. "You might be right. Planning hasn't always been my strong point. I'm more of an off-the-cuff sort of person. I just like to jump straight into things — like running a market stall." She placed a hand on one of the lily bouquets. "Even during my teaching career, I never really stuck to the lesson plans."

"Please try not to touch anything," said Tony, who was getting sweaty just watching her fingers brush over his petals.

"Oh," said Nesta, pulling her hand away. "I'm sorry." She turned to face his perfectly-trimmed beard. "You must be very patient to grow these beautiful flowers."

Tony's frown loosened and was happy to receive the compliment. "Yes, I suppose patience is part of it. I don't grow everything myself, but I do as much as I can. You have to have a system in place."

"Am I right in thinking that you used to be in the army?"

Nesta's question stunned him. Tony had presumed she was one of those annoying window shoppers, the kind who never intended to buy but liked to chat.

"Yes," he said. "How did you know that?"

"Dorothy."

Tony nodded. "That explains it."

"I wasn't too sure if she had you confused with someone else," said Nesta. "She seems a bit forgetful."

"Aye, Dorothy does suffer with her memory," said Tony with a heavy sigh. "Her long-term memory is still pretty good, though."

Despite her frustrating first encounter with this local woman, Nesta couldn't help but feel sorry for the woman. Memories were everything to Nesta, especially as she got older. She couldn't imagine losing *any* of them. "Were you in the army long?"

"Eighteen years," said Tony without any hesitation. "Welsh Guards."

"Welsh Guards?" Nesta prepared to study his reaction to her next sentence. "Then you probably knew Charlie."

Tony stared at her, giving away surprisingly little. "I knew Charlie Coogan, aye."

Nesta waited for further comment but none came. "Were you and him close?"

The florist turned his focus back on the stall and began

stacking up his boxes into equal piles. "We went to war together," he said, eventually. "That's about as close as a person gets. When your life is on the line, the people around you are like family."

"I'm sorry for your loss," said Nesta. Her condolences caused him to stop moving, and he took a moment to regain his composure. "The news must have come as a terrible shock."

"Yes," said Tony. "It was very unexpected."

"That's quite a coincidence, though — two fellow ex-soldiers working in the same market."

"Not really. Him and I used to share the same market stall."

Nesta nodded. She had hoped for a connection, but these two men had been more than just acquaintances, it had turned out. "Is that right?"

"Charlie had been working on the markets way before he joined the army, and he went straight back to his old ways as soon as he returned to civilian life. We both left the army after we got back from the Falklands."

"The Falklands?" Nesta asked, having wondered which war he had been referring to. He was too young for the ones that initially sprung to mind and too old for some of the more recent conflicts over the last few decades.

"We lost a lot of our regiment out there," Tony continued. "The ship we were on, the Sir Galahad, was struck on the way over. Charlie and I were lucky to make it out alive." A sadness swept over him. "A close friend of mine didn't make it."

"I'm sorry to hear that," said Nesta. "Was he from Mold?"

Tony nodded. He stared into the centre of a purple rose, as though it were a portal to the painful memories of the past. "We joined the army at the same time. It's all we ever wanted to do. As kids, we'd run around the Bailey Hill, shooting each other with sticks. Like a lot of kids, I suppose. But we never stopped dreaming. When I joined the army, I realised we weren't unique in that respect. A lot of the guys we served with had similar personalities — not all of them, mind. Don't get me wrong, there were plenty of people who signed up because they didn't know what else to do with their lives. But there are people out there who are natural soldiers — natural fighters. We were born to be warriors. I suppose it's in our nature as human beings. None of us would be here if our ancestors didn't know how to fight."

Nesta listened to every word with an open mind. She had never looked at it that way. The man had a point — war was a natural part of history. Nevertheless, she would have liked to think that mankind could move on from all that (as naive as she knew it sounded). Nothing ever good came from bloodshed.

"It must have been hard to move back into civilian life," she said, watching the self-proclaimed "warrior" tending to his flowers.

"You can say that again," said Tony. "Not only had I lost a friend, but I left the army as a broken man. It's not easy adjusting back into a small town when you've spent years being told what to do for every waking hour. The strict routine becomes a comfort after a while. The discipline never leaves you." He readjusted one of his flower pots. "I was a complete mess when I came back. Couldn't get a job, couldn't pay the bills. There was hardly any work, and I didn't have the skills or the qualifications anyway. I felt like an ex-convict. Can you believe that?"

Nesta gave him a sympathetic shake of her head. "What changed?"

Tony smiled. "I was walking through the market one Wednesday morning. I'd head to the job centre every day like clockwork. Job hunting had become a full time job in itself. I was religious about getting all the papers and checking the vacancies. That morning, I saw Charlie behind one of the stalls. He was selling these designer tracksuits. The guy was always keeping up with the trends. And that was when he offered me a job." His face lit up at the happy memory. "I was stubborn at first, obviously. But he managed to persuade me in the end. He went on to teach me the basics of running a small business. The main stuff, you know, gross profit margins, tax and all of that. I travelled all over North Wales with him. We sold allsorts. Eventually, I went on to start my own stall."

"What gave you the idea to sell flowers?" asked Nesta.

Tony turned to his colourful display with a sense of pride. "I was once told to find what you love and make a trade out of it. So I did. I always loved growing stuff in my back garden, especially flowers. I was never a vegetable grower. Too messy. Plus, you can't even see the root vegetables. I was always more of a meat eater anyway."

"You could have opened a butchers," said Nesta, glancing over towards Sean's meat truck. Her new archnemesis was busy laying out his precious cutlets.

Tony laughed. "Sean would kill me! No, I'll stick with the flowers. Much more satisfying."

"That was good of Charlie to help you out like that. Sounds like he was a good friend."

"Us army vets have always stuck together," said Tony. "I think Charlie felt like he owed me one."

"Owed you for what?"

The veteran smiled. "Saving his life."

CHAPTER 8

"He saved the guy's life?"

Darren had arrived early on his second day of working at the market, and his employer could not have been more surprised. After her conversation with Flower-Pot-Tony (a nickname that she had coined herself for her own amusement), Nesta had returned to her stall to find the eager teenager tapping his watch. When she explained the connection between Charlie Coogan and the man who ran the flower stall, Darren was curious to hear more.

"The two men had served together during the Falklands," Nesta continued.

"What's a Falklands?" asked Darren.

"A war that took place before you were born. Basically, Britain had to sail halfway across the world to take back some islands." She saw the young man's confused expression. "I know, I know. None of it will make any sense if I explain it now. But the point is — Tony Flower Pot —" Nesta paused to elaborate. "That's the man who sells the flowers."

"I gathered that," said Darren.

"Yes, well — Tony says that he saved a wounded Charlie

from drowning after their boat got hit. It sounds like they were both lucky to be alive."

Darren listened with an excited expression on his face. History had never been his strongest subject in school, but he had watched his fair share of Rambo films. He had also played the video game *Call Of Duty* many times over, which, as far as he was concerned, practically made him a war veteran himself.

"Do you know what weapons they were carrying?" he asked.

"Uh, no." Nesta gave him a curious look. "I didn't get a chance to ask him that one."

A disappointed Darren sighed. "Never mind, then." He looked down at the knitting. "So, what was your big plan to make us rich?"

Nesta smiled. She thought he would never ask.

Darren had to wait another twenty minutes before he found out the answer to his question. When Hari, Taylor and Kim arrived, the teenager soon wished he had never reminded her.

"Hold him steady," Nesta snapped, as she tried to adjust the miniature coat now wrapped around her Jack Russell.

Darren was less enthusiastic about this idea than the stubborn terrier, who had no desire to model his owner's clothing. "This is your genius idea?" he asked. "I did offer to model the knitwear myself. What makes you think the dogs are going to do any better?"

"Because," said Nesta, stepping back to admire her work, "people love looking at dogs. And if they love looking at dogs, then they'll be looking at our stall."

The teenager shook his head and did not share her optimism. "People love exotic birds. That doesn't mean we should set a load of them loose in front of the stall."

Nesta ignored him. "Right. Taylor, you're up next."

The cockapoo whimpered, before she was placed in her own

colourful, woollen straightjacket. Soon enough, all three of the furry volunteers were like a trio of woolly mummies.

"Aren't they adorable?"

A young woman with wide eyes and formal clothes came running over. Darren noticed her pretty features and jumped in front of Nesta to greet her. "That one's Taylor," he said. She's wearing part of our luxury range.

"Taylor?" the woman asked. "Like the singer? Oh, my God — I love her!"

"So do I!" Darren cried back.

Nesta rolled her eyes and shoved the teenager out of the way. "We're doing deals on a variety of sizes."

"Well," said the woman, "I don't own a dog myself, but my sister does, and she would love one! I'm late for my shift at the bank, but I can pop back on my break to buy one."

"I'm sure your sister will really appreciate that," said Nesta, turning to her assistant with a triumphant wink.

The once cynical teenager was forced to witness many similar encounters over the next hour, as customers of all ages headed over in their droves for a chance to look at the four-legged models and their new garments.

Unlike Hari, the cockapoos seemed to be enjoying the attention and took to the modelling like ducks to water.

"Who ever chose to name it a catwalk?" Nesta asked, clutching her handful of takings and slapping Darren on the back. She laughed in his baffled face. "*Dogwalk* more like!"

"People really do love their dogs," he muttered, as he exchanged another woolly coat for a wad of cash.

Even a suspicious Sean Lyons was taking regular looks from his meat van to see what all the fuss was about. Eventually, Nesta approached him with a smug face. "Got any sausages, Sean? The talent is hungry!" She lifted up her handful of notes and handed one over. "Keep the change, dear."

She returned to her stall with a look of horror, as her star cockapoos were now ripping each other's knitted coats to shreds.

"Darren!" Nesta cried. "Stop them!"

Her assistant could do very little to prevent even more carnage from unfolding, and the helpless teenager held his hands up in the air and watched the two dogs begin to inflict the same level of damage on Hari's woolly coat. It was hard to ignore Sean's amused howls over in the distance, whilst passing shoppers tried to keep their distance.

After doing their best to salvage the rest of their knitting stock before taking the dogs back home, an exhausted Nesta and Darren headed off for a much needed coffee break and took their hot drinks to the seclusion of St Marys' Church.

They approached the enormous building with a hesitation that was understandable for a recent crime scene, and the remains of shredded police tape could still be seen draped across the walled entrance.

The clock tower loomed above them, following their every move like an all-seeing eye.

Even Darren was struck by the church's formidable presence and took frequent glances at the tall, dark windows, as he followed Nesta around the outside.

They headed past countless names, all engraved into their individual stones. The teenager had always found graveyards rather disturbing (unlike his guide, who found them quite peaceful). Either way, the idea of death was far more prevalent than usual on this day. People rarely drew their last breaths in a graveyard and were normally dead long before entering them. Despite their deceased occupants, these isolated areas were probably the safest place a person could be. Unfortunately, this had not been the case for Charlie Coogan.

"He was lying over here," said Nesta, when they reached the exact spot she had found the man.

Darren walked over to the patch of grass and began filming it with his phone. Nesta had not missed his strange behaviour and turned her attention instead to the row of graves beside them.

"I wonder what he was doing here," she said, studying the names on the three headstones: Linda New, Edward Delyn, Robert Cain. "We should probably make a note of these names. Do you have a pen?" She watched Darren lift up his phone to take a quick snapshot of all three graves.

"Don't need a pen and paper," he said. "Job done."

A repulsed Nesta shook her head. "Can you at least *try* to have some respect for the people buried here?"

Darren turned to her with an innocent face. "How do you mean?"

"Well, this is a sacred place. You can't go around contaminating it with that machine of yours."

A sudden thought popped into the teenager's head. "Hey, do you think there are any ghosts around here?"

"Darren!"

"What?" He raised up his arms. "Ghosts love being caught on camera loads of times! I saw it on a *Tiktok* video."

Nesta wanted to bury her head alongside the graves. "You deserve to be haunted, young man."

"Maybe this Charlie's a ghost," Darren said. "It's always the murder victims. Maybe he can tell us who did it." He began looking around at their surroundings. There was a wall nearby with a large field on the other side. Perfect for someone to make a quick escape, he thought, and proceeded to film it with his phone. Next, he turned his lens upwards, towards the clock tower.

"Someone could get a decent shot from up there," he said.

Nesta groaned. "Don't start this sniper theory of yours again. There's no way that someone shot him from up there."

"They had to have shot him from *somewhere*." Darren mimicked a rifle in his hands and took an invisible shot. "It must have been a concealed area."

"Not necessarily," said Nesta. She walked a few feet away from him until her back was against the church wall. "Unless they indeed had a sniper rifle at their disposal, it's unlikely they were *that* far away to make the shot. Otherwise, their aim was impeccable."

"But Charlie would have seen who it was."

"Exactly. There's a strong chance that he knew who shot him. They could even have arranged a meeting."

"In a graveyard?"

Nesta shrugged. "There are stranger places. It's quieter than a *Costa*."

Darren shook his head. "I just don't see the point of using a gun unless you want to kill someone from a distance. Otherwise why not use a knife?"

"Knives are physical and risky." Nesta spoke as if she knew all about it. But, in reality, the closest she had ever come to hand-to-hand combat was wrestling with a broken washing machine. Still, she had watched plenty of Spaghetti Westerns and could get the gist of the whole thing. "A firearm is an almost sure-fire way to get the job done. Charlie might have been getting on a bit, but he was still an ex-soldier. You wouldn't want to mess around with a knife."

"Alright," said Darren. "Then why choose the outside of a church in broad daylight?"

Nesta smiled. "Why indeed. The location could be the key to everything. What was so special about the place?" She turned his attention to their surroundings: the church, the trees, the graves. "Maybe one of them was already here visiting someone."

Darren looked around again. "Like who? There hasn't been anyone around since we arrived."

"There's plenty of people here to visit," Nesta said, waiting for him to understand where her mind was heading.

The teenager gave her a confused frown. "Are you sure it's coffee in there?" He pointed to her paper cup.

Nesta rolled her eyes. "Why else do people come to a graveyard? Think flowers!"

"Ahhhh." The penny had finally dropped. "You think one of them was here to visit a grave?"

"It's possible..."

She walked over to the three gravestones where Charlie had been lying and studied the dates. "Well, one of these people died in nineteen-twelve. And you know what happened *that* year." Nesta turned around to see a blank expression. "The Titanic?"

"I never got round to watching the movie," said Darren. "Looks too long. I'm more of a short video kind-of-person. Less than thirty seconds, ideally."

The retired teacher tried not to groan in pain. "It was the year that the Titanic sank."

"What does that have to do with Charlie? Was he on board or something?"

"Nothing," Nesta snapped. "And no — he would not have been on board. My point was that this person is far too old to be visited by someone of Charlie's age — or any living person, really. They're not a parent — or a grandparent for that matter. So we can probably rule this person out."

"Maybe they're visiting a great great granny," said Darren, staring at the gravestone.

Nesta gave him a cynical frown. "Highly unlikely, sadly." It had struck her in that moment how sad it was that a person could be forgotten due to the passage of time. That a name could fade into obscurity as each generation passed, much like the fading name on a hundred-year-old gravestone. People could keep the memory of a grandparent alive, but it would all dissolve away as those grandchildren grew older, until they also became memories themselves. The harsh cycle of humanity, she thought. Nesta would have shared these morbid thoughts with Darren, but it was hard to discuss the realities of death with a teenager who liked watching strangers dance around on his mobile phone.

"These other two people," she said, moving back to the other gravestones. "Linda and Robert. They died a lot more recently."

Darren squinted at the dates carved into the stone and was just about to comment, when he realised someone was watching them. It was difficult to know how long this person had been standing behind them, but he didn't seem too pleased to see them.

CHAPTER 9

"Can I help you?"

The Reverend Colin Johnson was facing his two visitors with the face of a man who had experienced far too much stress in his life. Even at the age of twenty-nine, the young vicar was already losing his hair, and his complexion indicated that sunlight had not been a priority.

"Ah," said Nesta, reaching out her hand and forcing an immediate handshake. "We've met before — very briefly. The day Mr Coogan died, remember?"

Colin glanced at the teenager and breathed a sigh of relief. "Thank heavens. I thought you might have been those blasted reporters again."

"Reporters?" asked Nesta.

The vicar nodded. "The press have been pretty persistent." He acknowledged the enormous church looming beside them. "I suppose it's a great location. And a shooting indicates that this death was no accident." The man tried to loosen his collar and appeared to be suffering from a brutal hangover. "Forgive me if I startled you. I've been a bit on edge since I found Charlie's body. The gunshot didn't help. I get jumpy at the best of times."

"You knew Charlie?"

Colin squinted at the protruding sunlight coming down on him through the branches above them, like a vampire who rarely came outside. "Oh, yes. Charlie was a regular here at St Mary's."

Nesta was not overly surprised. She had a cousin who had served in the military, and he had also been a devout Christian. It wasn't hard to imagine how faith could have offered a much needed comfort when serving on the battlefield. "I didn't realise that he went to church here."

"Well," said the vicar. "It did take him a while." He chuckled to himself. "I first found Charlie out here in the graveyard, actually. Not that far from where we are standing now."

Nesta could feel Darren staring at her. "Oh? He was visiting a grave?"

"More than a few." Colin appeared to be a lot more relaxed than he had been upon his arrival. "He was looking for an ancestor of his. The man was working on his family tree."

"He was — *what*?" Darren's sudden question caused the other two to turn and face him. He struggled to hide his cynicism at the idea of someone taking the time to research their family history. Personally, he found his close family members hard enough and couldn't imagine trying to seek out more of them.

"I know," said Colin. "It sounds rather dull to a person of your age, I'm sure. But we all get more curious as we get older." He glanced down at his own immaculate shoes with a guilty expression. "Some of us take it a little further than others. I may have been a little guilty of that myself. Which is why we connected so well."

"How far back was he going?" asked Nesta.

"Goodness," said Colin. "We're talking generations. On both his father and mother's side." The man spoke with an accent that was far further south in origin than Flintshire, and he was certainly not a Mold native. "Although, he was far more interested in his mother's side."

Nesta watched the man's glasses slip down his sweaty nose. "Why's that?"

"There were a great deal from Mold. Apparently, the cemetery over near Tesco is full of his relatives. Charlie was very thorough. We once had an evening of wine and cheese to compare each other's ancestry. It had become somewhat of a hobby for me, too, and I introduced him to that *Lineage* website."

"The what?" asked Nesta.

"It's a website," said Darren. "My dad's on it all the time."

The word "website" had caused an immediate disinterest in the woman beside him, and she turned her attention back to the vicar.

"I was grateful for the company at the time," Colin continued. "I hadn't long moved here then. It's not easy settling into a new town when you don't know anybody." The vicar coughed. "If I'm being really honest, I was really struggling with my new position. I had been hoping for a small parish in a quiet, little village." He turned around and looked up at the enormous church. "St Mary's was a huge undertaking for my level of experience."

Darren scoffed and gazed around at their quiet surroundings. "Doesn't look too stressful to me. What happened? Run out of bread and wine?"

Nesta wanted to slap her young friend across the back of the head. Instead, she uttered his name in a disapproving tone. "Darren..."

The reverend laughed. "It's alright. I get it. How hard could it be, right? Well, when you're an introverted individual like me who doesn't take well to public speaking..." Colin paused and realised he was opening up far too much.

"I don't mean to be rude," said Nesta, who was surprised herself, "but was this really the right profession to choose, Reverend?"

Colin smiled and nodded. "It's preposterous, isn't it? The Lord likes us to test ourselves." He looked up to the sky full of clouds. "Don't get me wrong, I have always been very passionate from the theoretical standpoint. I've studied that bible inside and out. Theology has always fascinated me, and I am a man of true faith. But that doesn't mean I'm not human."

Nesta smiled. She appreciated his honesty and was starting to like the man. "I used to know plenty of school teachers who could sympathise. It's all well and good knowing your subject. But teaching a classroom of pupils is a whole other ball game."

The reverend nodded in appreciation. "Would you both like to come in for a little tour?" he asked.

"That would be wonderful," said Nesta, ignoring Darren's reluctant frown. "I love a good church."

It was true: Nesta had always enjoyed a good church. It was impossible — whether a person was a devout Christian or a sworn atheist — not to be mesmerised by these timeless pieces of architecture.

The exterior of this sandstone structure with its intricate details had been impressive enough, but it was the inside that truly excited Nesta. She entered with her head tilted back, taking in the vast size of this giant nave. The stained glass windows on either side of them were now glowing with colour and light, as the distinct smell of polish and burning candles reminded her of being in her own church back in Bala. It was all so familiar and yet quite different at the same time.

Even Darren was taking everything in with a pair of wide eyes, having only ever stepped foot inside a church once in his life as a boy. He glanced over at the enormous organ with its tall, metallic pipes and couldn't help but imagine a dastardly phantom character playing a rendition of Bach's "Toccata and Fugue in D minor" (not that he would have known the title or composer).

"Darren!" Nesta snapped, as she saw him filming away with his camera phone. "Will you stop that!"

Darren reluctantly lowered his phone and frowned. "What? It's not like it's a sin."

"It certainly should be. They really are the devil's work, those horrible devices." She waved her hands. "Can't you just enjoy the experience of seeing something with your own eyes?"

The teenager huffed. "Not if I can't post it afterwards. You know what they say — if it's not online, it didn't happen."

Nesta shuddered and tried not to let his chilling words ruin her experience. "Oh, look! It's the pulpit!" She pointed to the carved, wooden structure up ahead beside a section of choir stalls.

"A *what*?" asked Darren.

"Have you really never been inside a church before?"

"My Taid's funeral was in a church. But that's about it. I've got better things to do on my Sundays."

Nesta rolled her eyes. "Like watching cat videos?"

Darren scoffed. "Cat videos? How do you know about *them*? I thought you said you were only using your new phone for calls."

"I've only watched a couple," said Nesta. "They keep popping up." Her face blushed.

"It's called an algorithm."

"Anyway," Nesta snapped, trying to change the subject, "that's a very nice pulpit."

They followed the reverend all the way up to the altar. The proud vicar faced his invisible congregation and held up his arms. "It's quite something, isn't it?"

Nesta took a deep breath. "Oh, it's marvellous."

"It's definitely *something*," Darren muttered, checking on the video he had just filmed.

"You know," said Colin, "we're standing on the site of a Norman church. St Mary's, as we know it now, was re-built under the patronage of Henry VII's mother."

"How fascinating," said Nesta.

As Colin continued to divulge even more historical facts, Darren wandered off and climbed his way up to the pulpit. He raised up his arms, as though a crowd were hanging on his every word. "Hello, Cleveland! Let's get ready to rock!"

His voice echoed across the church, and he turned to the other two with a proud chuckle. An embarrassed Nesta buried her face in her hands and wished that an almighty power would part the ground beneath her and swallow her. She turned to the vicar and smiled. "It must be quite a sight to behold when it's full of people."

Colin nodded. "Why, yes. You should come along to one of our services."

Nesta genuinely considered his offer. "I might just do that. I'm in town for at least another week." She noticed a nearby eagle lectern with an open bible resting on its wings. The bird reminded her of the taxidermy she had seen at Charlie's stall and was glad this particular animal was made of wood.

"You said Charlie and you became quite close," she said after a moment of silence.

The vicar nodded. "Uh, yes. I suppose we did. The man had been looking to return to the church for years. His faith had been challenged for quite some time, and I think he was looking for answers."

"Did he find any?" asked Nesta.

"Well," said Colin. "I did my best to help. I gave him my honest take on the whole thing and it intrigued him."

"And what's that?"

The vicar smiled. "We'd need a lot more time than we have now, but I explained my relationship with God, how it helped me overcome some of my own personal issues over the years, how faith can be present even if you think it's gone." He paused and a sadness washed over him. "I lost both of my parents quite young, you see. I had a pretty bad relationship with loss and grief. I was very emotionally stunted for quite some time. Charlie was quite obsessed with the scriptures and the bible, and he had grown quite cynical of the whole thing. He'd quiz me on it all the time. Eventually, I had to explain that faith is not located in a load of ancient texts. It can come from the most inexplicable feelings. I used myself as an example. I was never religious growing up. But I remember being in my hall of residence in university. It was a cold winter's day, and I decided to take a walk. I don't know why. I found myself wandering the streets of London, aimlessly for hours, until I came across this church." Colin's eyes filled with warmth. "The door was ajar, and for reasons I could never explain, I decided to go inside. The place was as empty as this church is now, and I sat down on one of the benches. All of a sudden, this feeling came over me, and I could feel my parents sitting there beside me. There was nobody there, obviously, but that didn't matter. It was like a strange warmth that came over me, and I burst into tears. I don't know if the tears were happy or sad, but it was the most emotional I had ever been." The vicar turned to see that the woman beside him was listening intently, and he sighed. "I guess, what I was trying to explain was that, sometimes, it's just a feeling."

"I understand," said Nesta.

"I think Charlie did too," said Colin.

The vicar continued the rest of his tour, until he eventually excused himself and headed off into the back room.

Nesta and Darren were soon sitting next to each other in the middle of a central pew. The bored teenager sighed, as his companion began kneeling down and closing her eyes.

"Can we go now?" he asked.

Nesta gave him a sharp *hush*. "Can't you see I'm in the middle of something?"

"You don't look very busy." Daren pulled out his phone and began scrolling. All of a sudden, the sound of the church bell caused him to look upwards. "That would get annoying after a while." He waited for a response but realised that she was ignoring him. "Have you finished yet?" No response. "I should have got a video interview with that priest. He's *definitely* on the suspect list. The local vicars always are. And he was the only other person there at the scene of the crime."

"There were two people." Nesta's eyes remained shut.

"Did someone say something?"

"Two. There were two people outside when I found the body. Him and a groundskeeper."

Darren nodded. "We definitely need to speak to him again, then. Maybe they're *both* in on it." He heard a grunt and decided to ignore it. "Didn't you say that you also heard that bell go off?"

"It had just turned eleven o'clock," said Nesta, climbing up from her knees.

"How can you be certain?" asked Darren, who received an eyeroll.

"The giant clock on the outside of this building."

"Ah, yeah, right. Good point. We'll have to check if it's accurate, though."

Nesta scoffed. "It'll be more accurate than the one on that phone of yours."

Darren stared into his screen and was doing a full scan of the area on his online maps app. "See — there are a few places the shooter could have escaped. Here, here and here." A sudden thought popped into his head. "Hey! Do you think that vicar will show us how you get up that tower?"

The teenager looked up to see that Nesta had already left his side, and he was now alone in the middle of the church. "Hey! Wait for me!"

CHAPTER 10

The walk back from the church had been short but very pleasant. Nesta was returning to her stall with a newfound burst of motivation, and she was ready to do business again. After making her way through the busy crowds of the high street, she turned a corner to find a sight far more shocking than any dead body.

Gathered around her unattended market stall was a group of teenagers. With their similar style of clothing and almost identical haircuts, it was difficult to tell each one apart.

"Oi!!" Nesta cried out.

Two of the three teenagers had already bolted, whilst the remaining pair grabbed some more handfuls of knitting before making their own escape.

Nesta came running down the side street with flailing arms, and the thieves were long gone by the time she had reached her table.

As she tried to catch her breath, another figure went running past with determined strides. "Somebody grab them!" Darren cried out, honing his sights on one of the thieves. He quickened his pace, as the slowest of the group tripped up on a crate full of vegetables.

"I got you now!"

An excited Darren charged at his unsuspecting thief and pinned him up against a nearby wall.

"Get off!" the other teenager cried. "Get your hands off me!"

Darren made use of his extra size and continued to restrain the young man with a hold he had seen on a professional wrestling programme. The teenager known as Archie was a few years younger than his assailant and was lacking any noticeable muscle mass. Despite his disadvantage in weight, it didn't stop him from trying to escape.

"Where's the money box?" Darren asked. He shoved all of his weight in the direction of the wall, exhausting his captive until his wriggling subsided.

"I don't know what you're talking about!"

"It's alright." Nesta placed her hand on Darren's shoulder and encouraged him to loosen his tight grip. "I'll handle this."

Archie breathed a sigh of relief, until the senior citizen shoved her finger near his face and began berating him in a manner that only a former teacher could. "Now you look here! How dare you go around stealing people's things! Do you know how hard we market people work?"

The teenager looked back in terror. "I don't know what you mean — I didn't do anything!"

"Don't you lie to me, young man," Nesta growled. "Your parents would be ashamed. I'm sure they'd be shocked when I knock on your front door. Now, come on! Where are the goods?"

Archie emptied his pockets. "I told you! I ain't got nothing!"

"I haven't got anything, you mean!"

Now it was Darren's turn to step in, as he began fearing for the young man's safety. "I think he's telling the truth..."

"Him?!" Nesta snapped. "Tell the truth? Thieves don't go

around telling the truth! He knows exactly where my knitting is, and I'm going to find out."

"I didn't touch your stupid knitting! What would I do with some worthless bits of wool? Nobody's going to buy that!"

His words ignited a fire in Nesta's eyes.

"He's got a good point there," said Darren.

"Don't you start," Nesta snapped. "Those knitted animals are worth weeks of my precious time! And I'm not getting any younger!"

Archie took advantage of Darren's lapse in concentration and shoved his way free.

"You two are crazy!" he cried, before giving them an aggressive hand gesture.

Nesta watched the teenager scurry off and shook her head. "He wouldn't have dared do that in my class."

"We should never have left the money box," Darren muttered.

"At least they only took the animals," Nesta muttered back. "I can soon churn out more of them."

The teenager turned his head to glare at her. "I thought you said they were worth weeks of your precious time?"

Nesta shrugged. "Interrogation techniques, dear. You have to exaggerate a little, keep them on their toes."

"Does this belong to anyone?" asked a deep voice.

They both turned around to see Sean, the butcher, holding up a severed robin's head. Nesta cupped her own mouth, as she saw the cotton wool poking out from her robin's neck.

"Oh, those monsters." She took the head from him and held it gently.

"Plenty more where that came from," said Sean with an amused smirk. He pointed back towards Daniel Owen square. "Someone dumped a load of it back down that way."

Darren saw Nesta's fist turn a bright shade of white, as she squeezed the robin's head with all of her might.

"I know what we need," he said, turning her around and walking them both back towards the stall.

"And what's that?" Nesta growled.

Darren smiled. "A nice coffee. Let me grab us some." He checked his pockets. "Any chance you could lend me a fiver?"

∼

DARREN APPROACHED the humming barista with a slight tingle of nerves in his stomach. He had noticed her face and distinctive purple hair on the very first day and had been waiting for an excuse to make contact. Granted, she seemed a few years older than he was, but that hadn't stopped Nick Jonas.

His gentle coughs had done nothing to catch Claire's attention, and he was forced to blurt out a noise so horrid that it made him choke on his own saliva.

"Oh," she said, looking up from her coffee machine. "Are you alright?"

Darren tried to recover, but his eyes had already started to water. "Uh, yeah. All good over here, like. How about you?"

She handed him a napkin for his excess saliva. "I'm doing just fine. What can I get you?"

The young man stared at the beautifully arranged drinks menu and, just like his older companion, struggled to make sense of most of it. "I'm finding it hard to choose. It all looks so good."

"You like coffee?" asked Claire.

"Oh, yeah. I'm a bit of a connoisseur, actually."

"Is that right?"

"Yeah, yeah, yeah. I'm well into coffee, me. *Nescafé, Kenco, Maxwell House...*" He paused for effect. "*Nescafé Alta Rica.*"

Claire tried to keep a straight face. "Wow, South American coffee. So how would you like your coffee on this fine day, Mr Barista?"

Darren let out a smug grin. "Milk, two sugars, please."

The young woman began preparing his drink. "Don't I recognise you from somewhere?" she asked, eventually.

"Ah," said Darren, holding his head up high. "You've probably seen me online. I'm a bit of an influencer. I've got my own *YouTube* channel. It's pretty popular."

Claire shook her head. "Nah, I remember now. You're the one with that knitting stall and the cockapoos! God, they were so cute."

Although slightly disappointed by the point of reference, he was happy to be associated with anything "cute". "Oh, right. Those are my dogs, yeah."

"They looked so adorable in those little coats," Claire continued. "And your friend is so lovely."

"Friend?" Darren asked, struggling to contain his embarrassment.

"Your business partner. She a mate of yours?"

Darren could feel his face turning red. "Oh, no, she's not a — she's my granny." He forced out a laugh. "Mate? No! I got loads of mates my own age. I'll be chilling with those dudes later."

"You're her grandson?"

"Yeah, I'm just helping her out on the stall."

"That's so sweet of you." Claire popped a lid on his hot beverage. "That's a really nice thing to do."

The teenager jiggled his head again. "Yeah, well, I'm a caring person, I suppose." He pointed at the coffee machine. "I'll get another one of those for her, too."

Claire nodded and began moving her hands at a speed that her customer struggled to keep up with. He watched her effortlessly prepare the coffee granules like a flamboyant cocktail mixer. "So what's this channel of yours?"

Darren was in the middle of taking a sip of his hot drink and felt the tip of his tongue burn. "It's a true crime channel. Like a podcast but with videos and interviews and location footage and stuff. You should check it out."

"Maybe I will," said Claire. "I love a good podcast. You find there's enough crime in North Wales?"

"Enough," said Darren. "I travel around, though, looking for new cases."

"Any grisly murders?"

"A couple. There was this one murder in Bala." He turned around and nodded his head in the direction of the church. "And obviously..."

"Oh, yeah!" Claire took her eyes off the machine for a moment but her hands kept going. "Old Charlie!"

"You know him?"

She struggled to hide her contempt. "Sadly, yes. He's a friend of my grandad's. Proper military type. Not my kind of guy."

"What *is* your type of guy?" Darren saw her surprised face and instantly regretted his question. "Uh, what I mean is — what *didn't* you like about him?"

Claire smiled and enjoyed watching him squirm. "Let's just say I've always been somewhat of a rebel. The army doesn't like people like me. And I should know with generations of military people in my family. I'm more of a free spirit."

"That's a lot like me," said Darren. "I'm not big on the rules."

The barista nodded and pointed to her coffee trailer. "As you can see, I can take my business wherever the wind blows. A bit like you. What is it they call it? A digital nomad?"

"That's me." If Darren had been wearing a cowboy hat, he would have tipped it. "I'm actually not from around these parts. Just passing through. What about you?"

Claire chuckled. "I'm very much from Mold. But I get around. I'm actually saving up for my very own campervan. Then I'll *really* be free."

Darren grinned. This person was unlike anyone he had come across in his hometown of Bala, and her dream of living on the road certainly appealed to him. He had read about such lives in the pages of his heavy metal magazines, where musicians traveled from town to town without a care or worry in the world. Perhaps coffee was more rock and roll than he had thought.

"Hey," he said. "We should do a video for the channel together."

Claire's eyebrow rose up as if elevated by the steam from her coffee machine. "You want to film me for a true crime channel?" She didn't know whether to be disgusted or flattered. "That's probably the creepiest thing anyone's ever asked me. What kind of videos are you making?"

Her unexpected reaction to his proposal alarmed the young man, and he raised up his hands in defence. "No, no! It's nothing like that — I didn't mean —" He failed to notice her playful smile. "You said it yourself — that Charlie was a mate of yours."

Claire scoffed. "He most certainly was *not* a mate."

"We could just have you doing a segment to camera, talking."

"About what?"

"Anything you can think of. It doesn't all have to be a hundred percent accurate. The viewers don't care."

"Wow," said Claire. "So it's one of those true crime channels. Where truth blurs with fiction."

"Exactly!"

Despite him not noticing her disapproving tone, she admired his enthusiasm. She always respected passion, no matter how ludicrous the person was.

"Well," she said, flicking back her hair like a Golden Age film star. "I guess that performing arts course wasn't completely wasted."

"You're a performer?" Darren was beginning to realise that this barista with a trailer was full of surprises, and he couldn't believe his luck. The only thespian he had filmed so far was a farmer from Bala who enjoyed amateur dramatics.

"I've been known to tread the boards," said Claire, waving her arms around like a mime artist. "I did an interactive theatre performance in *The Dolphin* once."

"That's great," said Darren. "We can arrange a time. Maybe afterwards... I can buy you dinner..."

Claire laughed. "Don't worry about that. This one's free of charge."

The young man felt his neck getting hot before it carried up towards his cheeks. "Oh, no, I meant —"

"Hey! There you are!" Claire waved at the young woman approaching them. She grabbed hold of her, and they both kissed.

Darren witnessed the entire exchange with a stunned face.

The two women turned to him with a smile.

"This is Jen," said Claire. "My gorgeous other half."

"Hey, young man," said Jen, pointing to her girlfriend. "This young lady hasn't been ripping you off, I hope!"

"Hi," said Darren, raising his hand up as though it was frozen.

"Look who else it is!" The barista waved at a man carrying an armful of flowers. "Hi, grandad!"

Darren turned to find her addressing a familiar market trader. "*That's* your grandad? The flower stall guy?"

"Now *there's* a name I bet he never thought he'd have back in the day," said Claire. "The flower guy!" She laughed and wandered off with her partner.

Darren continued to stand there with a coffee in each hand, as he watched Tony Cockle making his way back to his flower stall. She really *was* full of surprises, he thought.

CHAPTER 11

"Well *you* took your time!" Nesta felt like she had been waiting an eternity for a coffee by the time her assistant had returned back to the stall.

Darren handed her the drink, and she went in for the first sip. "It's stone cold! What on earth have you been doing?"

The teenager blushed. "I was on a reconnaissance mission," he said, looking around to make sure that nobody was listening (and they weren't).

"Don't you start getting all army on me," Nesta snapped. She took another sip and winced. "All I wanted was a hot drink — not a spy."

"I was gathering info on the Charlie Coogan case," said Darren.

"Which is about as cold as this frappuccino!"

"I think it might be a flat white —"

"I don't care what it's called — as long as it's hot and caffeinated!"

They both sipped their drinks in silence for a moment, watching the shoppers pass by whilst not taking any notice.

"You'll never guess what I heard," Darren said, eventually. There was a pause, but he knew she couldn't resist. Then came the sigh.

"Go on..."

"You know your flower man? Tony? He's only that barista's grandfather."

Nesta scoffed. "That's hardly surprising in a small town. I'm sure there are plenty of connections."

"She doesn't like Charlie," Darren continued. "In fact, I think she hated him."

"Enough to shoot the man in the chest?" asked Nesta. "Gosh, if everyone who didn't like someone then killed them, there wouldn't be many of us left." She glanced over at the butcher van. "This town would certainly have a meat shortage for a while. Besides, Charlie seemed to have rubbed a lot of people up the wrong way."

Darren blew across the lens of his camera phone and rubbed it. "Well, she's agreed to do a video for the channel."

"*Has* she now? Well, that's classic murderer behaviour — kill someone and then record a public video about the man. It's hardly lying low."

"I never said she murdered the man," said the teenager. "But it would be *genius* if she had. Nobody would expect it." He began studying their counter. "What's the damage like? Did they take everything?"

"More than we've sold," said Nesta. "Which isn't saying much. Fortunately, I prepared a lot of extra stock." She pulled out a giant box from underneath the table and caught sight of a woman walking past them with a vinyl record underneath her arm. "That reminds me," she said, patting her assistant on the back. "How about you hold the fort for a bit and unload some of those boxes."

Darren watched her heading off. "Where are *you* going?"

"To buy a record!" Nesta called back.

∼

MARK HUTSON'S record stall was a trip down memory lane for anyone curious enough to browse its vast selection of second-hand vinyl. Nesta was one of these volunteers, and she flicked through the range of colourful covers with pure delight. It was easy to see how such a music format had still kept its place in the public's heart.

"See anything you fancy?" asked Mark, chewing on his stale gum.

Nesta continued her search, until she landed on a familiar face that made her smile. "Ah, here's a good one."

Mark wandered over to have a look. "Elvis Presley? At Christmas?"

"I could listen to those songs any time of year," Nesta said. "My late husband was a huge fan, you see. He used to collect stamps of him and everything. The king was always playing in our house."

"People do like to collect some strange things," said Mark, looking out at the busy high street. "I suppose stamps aren't that unusual."

Nesta clutched the Christmas hits album tightly in her arms like a warm blanket. "Elvis was there for our first proper date together."

Mark turned his head in surprise and lowered his designer sunglasses. "Seriously? You saw Elvis on your first date?"

Nesta coughed. "Well, he was an Elvis tribute act, technically." Her eyes sparkled at the memory. "And he sounded just like him, he did. Bala Golf Club. I remember that night as if it was yesterday. Elfyn Presley. He also worked at the bakery. Talented lad, that one."

A disappointed Mark lowered his glasses. "I've done a bit of Elvis impersonating myself."

"Have you really?"

"Only a bit, like. When I was first starting out in showbusiness." Mark pulled out a cigarette and lit up. "I was with this agency for a while who used to specialise in them. They even had a chubby one!" He let out a laugh. "But I didn't want to be an impersonator forever. I saw what happened to *those* guys, and it's not a pretty sight."

"So you sing your own songs now?" asked Nesta.

Mark smiled. He thought she would never ask. "Have yourself one of these to go with your Christmas carols," he said, scurrying over to grab a plastic CD case from a nearby box.

Nesta gazed down at the cover and saw a serious looking Mark with three other middle-aged men lined up beside him. It reminded her of a police line-up, and the fact that it was black and white didn't help. "Is this your band?"

"The Gaggles. Our greatest hits." Mark let out a proud grin. "Consider it a gift. Nothing like spreading the joy of my music around."

Nesta clutched the plastic case in her hands and gave him a polite nod. She wasn't even sure if she still owned a CD player, but there might have been something in the attic. "Why, thank you very much. My friend will probably enjoy this."

"Does he appreciate good music?" asked Mark.

"He's very young," said Nesta.

Mark nodded. "That's good. It's important to educate the new generation. Him and his mates will love it." A sudden thought popped into his head. "Hey, how long are you in town for?"

Nesta had to think about it. Her first week had flown by and a lot had happened so far. "At least another week."

The record dealer handed her a flyer with the title: Mold

Rockamania. "Me and the boys are playing there tomorrow. Daniel Owen Square. We do it every year. You should come down."

"Oh," said Nesta, staring at the bright colours. The last live gig she had attended was over near Talacre beach, and it hadn't exactly been the most relaxing evening out she had ever had. "I'm afraid I've already got plans."

"Another gig?" asked Mark.

"Sort of. I suppose it is a live event, and there *will* be music. The organiser invited me to come along."

"Is it a decent venue?"

Nesta smiled. "Absolutely. It's St Mary's Church."

The man's face dropped, and he began to chuckle. "Don't you worry about that." He patted the flyer. "This starts in the afternoon. You'll have plenty of time. Bring some mates."

"Actually, I do have a friend who likes his rock and roll..." Nesta pictured Darren's excited face when he heard the news.

"Perfect!" Mark clapped his hands.

They both looked up to see a fellow market trader heading towards them. Samir Mandal possessed the widest range of shoes known to man. He sold everything, from designer trainers to formal shoes, and his stall had always done well in Mold. But, on this occasion, the object in his hand was not a shoe; it was the remains of a knitted penguin.

"I tried to save him for you," said Samir. "But there was nothing we could do."

Nesta gave him an appreciative smile and took the penguin back with a heavy heart. "He was one of the unlucky ones."

"Those rotten youngsters," Samir said, shaking his head. "Those four are always up to no good. I'm always having to keep an eye on them."

"Specifically those four?" asked Nesta.

Samir nodded. "There are others, but the four I saw at your stall today are usually the main culprits for theft around here."

"The Fab Four," said Mark with a laugh. "Hey, you know who was a massive Beatles fan?" He turned their attention to the empty space opposite his stall. "It's still strange not to see him standing there. Charlie had that spot for years. Him and I had to look at each other all day."

"Charlie was a Beatles fan?" asked Nesta. She was genuinely surprised without knowing exactly why. The army veteran seemed more like a Rolling Stones fan. Or something more akin to Frank Sinatra.

"Only the biggest fan I've ever met," said Mark. "I bet he'd give your husband a run for his money."

Nesta scoffed. "I very much doubt it. My Morgan was fanatical."

"So was Charlie. He was always rooting through my records, looking for a Beatles album. The guy said he owned a shirt that Ringo Star once wore during the *Magical Mystery Tour*. He'd apparently spent years trying to track it down and had to buy it from some ex-bodyguard of theirs. Lord only knows if the shirt was genuine, but he thought it was. He even showed it to me once."

"And what was it like?" asked Nesta.

Mark shrugged. "Like an old shirt." He smirked. "He collected allsorts of memorabilia, Charlie did. But the real Holy Grail for him was a rare vinyl record."

"Sounds like he came to the right place," said Samir.

"You would think so," said Mark. "But this was something else." He looked around and lowered his voice, as though he was about to share the whereabouts of the Holy Grail itself. "Back in nineteen-fifty-eight, The Beatles — or The Quarrymen as they were then called — recorded their first ever record. There were two songs: a cover of Buddy Holly's 'That'll Be the Day' on one side and the first ever Beatles song on the other — 'In Spite Of All The Danger'. Now, the story goes that only one copy was pressed, which ended up in the hands of McCartney himself. But it turns out, according to Charlie, that there was a second press — another disc out there that the record company kept for himself."

His two listeners were completely captivated at this point and were dying to hear more about this tall tale of Charlie's.

"Is the story true?" asked Samir.

"Charlie was adamant that it was," said Mark. "And I even tried to help him track it down at one point."

"Did you have any luck?" asked Nesta, hoping for a positive answer.

Mark smiled. "I had this contact in Liverpool. Seedy bloke, to be honest, but he knew his vinyl. I'm pretty sure the guy used to be a bit of a gangster back in the day. I then introduced him to Charlie, and he went down a bit of a rabbit hole with the whole thing." He shook his head. "That man was pretty determined once he set his mind to something, I'll give him that."

"What was in it for you?" Nesta asked.

"A rather handsome finder's fee." Mark jiggled his head like a bobble doll. "That was the deal from the start. Me and Charlie were hardly mates. This was strictly business."

"Well?!" Samir cried out, overcome by the anticipation. "Did he find the record?"

"He found a record," said Mark. "Trouble is, it was a fake. The other problem was, he didn't realise that until he got home with it." The man sniggered. "He was absolutely livid. You should have seen him on the next market day — he came marching up to my stall and clobbered me with it."

"Yes," said Samir. "I remember that day. We thought he'd lost his marbles."

Mark huffed. "I think he lost those a long time ago."

"Did he get his money back?" asked Nesta.

The record dealer looked at her as though she was a naive child. "There's no refunds in this business. And you wouldn't want to accuse that bloke in Liverpool of being a crook. He had a lot of unpleasant mates."

"So he *was* a crook?"

"Yeah, I suppose he was." Mark held up his hands. "But you can't shoot the middle man."

Nesta was struck by his use of the word "shoot". It was a poor choice of word considering Charlie's demise.

"Ronnie!" Mark cried, as one of his regular customers approached the stall. He excused himself and left the other two to dwell on this tale of mystery and betrayal.

"That was a disappointing ending," said Samir. "I was hoping he found the record."

"Maybe he did," said Nesta. "I guess we'll never know." She lifted up her battered penguin. "Thanks again for Jeremy."

"Jeremy?" asked Samir.

Nesta blushed. "I like to name all of my knitted animals. Something I used to do back on the farm when I was a little girl. You can imagine my father's horror when he found out all of his livestock had names."

Samir shook his head in dismay. "I'm so sorry about those little thieves. You're lucky Charlie wasn't around — he would have hunted them down!"

She turned to him with curious eyes. It was hard to tell whether the man was joking, and she suspected by the genuine amusement in his face that perhaps he wasn't. "Did Charlie ever get anything stolen?"

"I'm sure we all have at some point," Samir muttered. "It comes with the territory, especially with that gang around.

They're the worst I've seen." He chuckled. "But they probably wouldn't dare steal from Charlie."

"No?"

The shoe salesman shook his head. "He had something of a reputation in this town for taking the law into his own hands."

"He was a vigilante?" asked Nesta. She couldn't help but think of a certain caped crusader running around the streets of Mold tackling crimes. Embarrassingly, it was not the version played by Christian Bale or Michael Keaton (she was more of an Adam West fan). In many ways, she was somewhat of a crime fighter herself (if solving murders could count) and couldn't help but picture herself wearing colourful tights and sporting a nice cape. Some fantasies in life were best kept to a person's private thoughts, she had decided, and never to be spoken aloud in public.

"Let's just say that Charlie had some very strong opinions about tackling local crime," said Samir. "He was quite old school and his army background probably contributed to that. He used to compare criminals to pests. And just like a pest control person, you couldn't tackle a problem lightly."

"Goodness," said Nesta, genuinely shocked. "As the widow of a former police officer, she had her own opinions on crime prevention, but she did not condone any form of violence. "Did you know Charlie well?"

"He lived on my street," said Samir. "The posher end, of course. On Clwydian Road."

"Posh? You mean, he had a nice house?"

Samir chuckled. "You can say that again. Alyn House — a beautiful detached house at the end of my road. It definitely gives my bungalow a run for its money. I think it's Edwardian."

"Maybe there's more money in this market game than I thought," said Nesta, thinking about her empty money box.

"I wish!" Samir cried. "Charlie came into some inheritance

money before he moved to Mold. It was his mother's, I believe. A small fortune. He apparently owned the house outright. I think he just kept working the markets to keep himself busy. I hear a lot of veterans are the same way. You have to keep moving."

"I know the feeling," said Nesta. Her retirement had been hard enough for a former teacher to adjust to. She certainly understood the need to keep busy.

"He was an interesting neighbour," said Samir. "Even though he was quite a few doors down. He once tried to get the whole road to join his little neighbourhood watch society. A couple of people were very much on board with his way of thinking. But it was far too extreme for me. I think fear and self-preservation make ordinary people resort to some strange things."

"What sort of things?"

Samir looked at her and suddenly became very aware of all the people around them. He may have shared a bit too much, he thought. "Let's just say that a lot of it was scare tactics. There was nothing too crazy." The man looked over towards his stall and saw that his wife was struggling. He excused himself and left Nesta to the wonders of her imagination.

"Hey!" cried a voice.

Nesta turned to see Claire making her way along the street. The barista waved and headed over.

"Hello," said Nesta.

"I got to meet your grandson earlier," said Claire. "You must be very proud."

"Grandson?"

"Yeah, you know — teenager, long hair, Metallica t-shirt, good taste in music. You two are drinking me out of coffee today."

Nesta's face soured. "He said I was his *grandmother*?" Her confusion surprised the barista, who was beginning to regret her little detour back to the coffee trailer.

"He said he was helping you out," Claire added. "I said it was very sweet of him. Wish I was that close with my granny!"

"I feel very lucky," said Nesta, clenching her fists. All of a sudden, the furious woman was keen to return to her knitting stall. She had a bone to pick with a certain teenager, and it was a very large one indeed.

CHAPTER 12

"So what record did you buy?" asked Darren. The woman beside him had not said a word since she returned to the stall, and he was beginning to think that something was wrong. Normally, he had the opposite problem, and she continued her silent protest by merely handing him a carrier bag.

The teenager rummaged inside and pulled out a record that made him scoff. "*Elvis*?! Really?"

"Oh," said Nesta. "I'm sorry. Do you have a problem with the greatest artist of all time?"

Darren detected an iciness in her tone, but at least she was speaking to him now. "And what's this?" He pulled out a copy of Mark's album and laughed.

This time, Nesta was genuinely a little embarrassed and snatched the CD case from him. "They're a new indie band, actually. They might be too underground for you."

"They look about as underground as an Eagles tribute band," said Darren with a snigger. "There's more denim in that album cover than a cowboy's trouser drawer."

"That's a little rich coming from you, Mr Metalhead."

Darren saw the disdain in her face. "Have I done something?" he asked. "You're acting all funny."

"Well," said Nesta, folding up her arms. "Maybe that's how old grannys are supposed to act."

"Granny?" The confused teenager suddenly had a memory of a recent conversation and began to feel uncomfortable.

"That's what you called me, isn't it? How old do you think I am? Or were you just embarrassed..."

"You've been talking to that barista," said Darren. He saw her furious scowl and threw his arms in the air. "I didn't want to weird the girl out, okay?"

"Why would she feel weird?" asked Nesta.

"Look at us!" Darren cried. His loud voice caused a passing gentleman to stare, and they both smiled at him until he disappeared. "We're *weird*!"

"I would speak for yourself," Nesta muttered.

"How many teenagers do you know who hang around with a pensioner all day?" He saw her begin to ponder his question. "I mean, you're an ex-teacher for God's sake! The whole thing's mental!"

Nesta nodded. It was certainly unusual. She could give him that. "So why *are* we hanging around together?"

"I've no idea!" Darren cried. He saw the hurt in her eyes and let out a sigh. "Because, maybe, sometimes — two weird things make a right."

"I am most certainly not weird," said Nesta.

Darren scoffed. "You bloody well are!"

They both gazed down at the selection of knitting in front of them.

"I thought you came to Mold so you could make some extra money," Nesta said, eventually.

"I did," said Darren. He lifted up the money box and shook it at her. "But that's not gonna happen, is it?"

Nesta laughed. "I've not given up hope yet."

The teenager let out another sigh and shrugged. "Honestly? If I wasn't standing here right now, I'd just be killing time on Bala high street. I guess, what I'm trying to say is —"

"Life is more interesting when you're hanging out with Nesta Griffiths?" Nesta gave him a warm smile.

He smiled back. "Well, it's slightly less boring, anyway."

"How charming."

"Plus," said Darren, lifting up his phone. "I'd have a lot less views on my channel. As they say in the online media world — content is king."

"Always happy to oblige." Nesta rolled her eyes. "I'd hate for the internet to have less content."

They stared at the crowds of people for a while with an awkward silence.

"So," Nesta continued. "Are you trying to tell me that we make a good team?"

Darren turned to her and cringed. "*Team*?"

"Isn't that what we are?"

"I have no idea *what* we are. I guess it is what it is."

Nesta nodded. She was happy with that conclusion.

"Oh," Darren added, reaching into his pocket, "I've been meaning to tell you..." He lifted up a five-pound-note.

"What's that?" asked Nesta.

The teenager let out a proud grin, as though he had been sitting on this big reveal all along. "Money for one of the baby cardigans."

The woman's eyes widened in front of him. "We made a sale?"

Darren nodded before Nesta grabbed him by the scruff of the neck and pulled him in tight for a hug. "Alright, alright! Calm down! Not in front of the customers!" His pleading cries were drowned out by the woman's happy squeals, as she refused to let him go whilst jumping up and down with excitement.

"We made a sale! We made a sale!"

Shoppers smiled as they walked past, and the embarrassed teenager could only take so much.

"Why didn't you put the money in the tin?" Nesta asked, once she had let her helpless victim go.

Darren tidied up his ruffled hair. "I thought it would spoil the surprise."

"Well," said Nesta, reaching into her own pocket. "I also have a little surprise for you —" She pulled out Mark Hutson's flyer and handed it to him. "Tah-dah! Tomorrow afternoon, Daniel Owen Square — my treat! Tickets are on me."

A concerned Darren stared at the large writing. "*Rockamania*?"

"I thought you'd love it. With your Metal-thingies and Guns and Posey's."

"You know there's a big difference between heavy metal and — whatever this stuff is!" Darren lifted up the flyer. He could see the enthusiasm in the woman's face and felt that similar tingle of emotion that he'd felt earlier (it might have been a form of guilt or pity, but he wasn't quite sure). "That's very kind of you, but — this is tomorrow. There's no buses back to Bala on Sundays."

"Then you can stay at my daughter's house," said Nesta. "I'm sure your father won't mind if we let him know. I also had some other ideas..." She gave him a mischievous look and it disturbed him greatly. "Charlie Coogan's house."

"Come again?"

"Tonight," she said. "We could go take a look. One of the market traders I spoke to earlier said he lived on the same street. The house is very photographic, I hear." She pointed down at his phone. "You could maybe get some nice footage."

Darren's concerned face began to brighten. Now, Nesta had spoken his language, and she was just about to seal the deal.

"We could put this towards a nice pub meal," Nesta continued, waving the five-pound-note in the air as if it were a cheque from the *National Lottery*.

The teenager could feel his stomach rumbling already. The only meal he had waiting for him back in Bala was a frozen lasagne.

"Hello? Does anybody work here?"

They both looked up to see Dorothy hovering over their items.

"Oh," said Nesta. "I'm very sorry, madam. This young man will be more than happy to go through our entire range with you, won't you, Darren? He's our best salesman."

Darren was suspicious of her sudden enthusiasm but obliged with a shrug. "Uh, yeah, I guess."

"That's good," said Dorothy. "I got a lot of questions."

Nesta patted her assistant on the back and prepared to excuse herself for the next half hour. "Don't you worry, Dorothy," she said with a wicked smile. "You take your time. Darren will be happy to help."

CHAPTER 13

"There you go, love. Don't forget to heat it up when you get home. It's the only way!"

Simon Rogers winked at his regular and handed her one of his deep filled pies. The bakery stall owner sidestepped his way to the next customer, who was ready with her loaf of bread. "That'll be three pounds if you've got it."

Nesta handed the man her coins and became distracted by something very appetising in the corner of her eye.

"Ah," said Simon. "See you've got a sweet tooth like me."

"A *Manchester tart*?" Nesta asked. "I've never heard of such a thing."

The man opposite her dropped his elbow down on the counter and held his chin. "Are you being serious? Never heard of one? Madam! That's despicable."

Nesta couldn't help but smile. "Are you sure you've not just made it up?"

"Manchester tarts have been around forever!" Simon licked his lips. "My mother used to make one every Saturday. Two of your five-a-day, she used to say with a giggle!"

His customer sighed. "Well, now I'll simply have to take one of those as well. Then I've tried everything."

The man clapped his hands. "That's the spirit! You won't regret it!"

Nesta waited for him to wrap up her tart and took a quick peek at the cake stall further down the street. "Just don't tell Wendy. Or she'll shoot me."

Simon scoffed. "Wendy? She'll more likely chop you up with a cake knife than end it quickly with a gun. Although, who knows at the moment when it comes to this place. It's like the wild west with all these guns going off."

They both looked over towards the church, which stood tall over in the far distance with its rectangular clock tower.

"It's shocking," said Nesta.

"Not *that* shocking," said Simon. "Not that he was killed by a firearm, anyway. The bloke had plenty of them."

"Excuse me?" Nesta was quite familiar with the job description of an army soldier, but she did not realise that they had a tendency to take their work home with them.

"Oh, yeah." Simon pulled out a tooth pick and began prodding the inside of his mouth. The chain around his neck glimmered in the sunshine, as did the enormous watch dangling from his wrist. "Charlie was armed to the tooth."

"He was?"

"All vintage, obviously. The bloke was always going on about his old gun collection."

Nesta had come across very few firearms in her time, except the rifles on her parents' farm. "I thought Charlie collected Beatles memorabilia?"

Simon laughed. "The man collected everything! Guns, records, sporting memorabilia — you name it. It was the only thing we had in common really."

"You collect guns?" Nesta asked.

Simon laughed even harder. "Guns? Me? God, no. Not unless they were a real antique. I'm always on the lookout for anything special. Aren't I, Jake?!" His call was overheard by Jake, his teenage son. "I love a good find!"

Jake shook his head. "Junk, you mean!"

"He loves it," said Simon with a snigger. "I've always had a habit of bringing stuff home with me. Can't help myself."

"What kind of things?"

"Clocks at the moment." The man stood tall with pride. "I go through phases. But clocks can be really valuable if you find the right ones."

"They're junk!" Jake cried out.

The heckles did nothing to dampen Simon's spirits. "One man's junk is another man's fortune, remember, son?" He turned back to Nesta. "Bargain hunting's in our DNA when it comes to our line of work." He looked around at his fellow market traders, all busy hustling their way to the next sale. "Shoes, bread, sweets — it's all the same. You have to always be on the lookout for other ventures. Things are changing all the time. If we don't evolve, we die." He let out a grin that exposed a gold tooth. "You got to keep your eyes and ears to the ground."

"I think you'll be alright," said Nesta, looking down at his baked goods. "People will always need their carbs."

"As do I!" Simon cried, patting his large pot-belly. "But I wasn't always selling bread."

"No?"

The man pointed at some of his contemporaries. "You take a look at all the people on this street. You'll find that most of them have changed trades. Take Samir, over there —" They both looked towards the shoe stall. "He used to sell hair products."

Nesta stared at the balding man with great interest. "How surprising."

"Yep," Simon continued. "He moved literally from his head to his feet. And has never looked back."

"So why aren't you selling antiques?" Nesta asked.

Simon scoffed. "That's more of a hobby nowadays." He pulled a smug face. "You know I've been on *The Antiques Roadshow* twice?"

His impressed customer gasped. Nesta could hear the trumpeting theme music sounding in her ears. "Have you really? My husband and I used to love watching that programme. We'd try and guess the value of each item. Both of us were always way off."

"Sadly," Simon muttered, "on both occasions, I was bitterly disappointed. But my porcelain doll got me at least a hundred quid."

"What's the secret?" Nesta asked. "To finding a priceless antique?"

The man lifted up his cap and smiled. He thought she would never ask. "Car boot sales."

"Really?" Nesta had expected something far more elaborate, like raiding a temple with a cowboy hat and bullwhip, or something of that nature.

"Oh, yeah. That's where you find all the hidden gems. People have no idea what they're throwing out half the time."

"Why do I get the impression you have a very untidy house?" Nesta asked.

Simon grinned. "Have you been talking to my other half? Yeah, I suppose our garage does need a good sort out. But it's apparently nothing compared to that Charlie's house." The man waved at a passing regular. "Charlie lived alone, you see. In a big house. Plenty of room."

"I thought army people were supposed to be organised and tidy?"

"I think some people fall into bad habits over time. Like

those ex-footballers or boxers who get all fat. Once you take your foot off the pedal, there's no going back."

His son threw a scrunched-up paper bag towards his stomach and called out: "When did you ever put your foot *on* the pedal?"

Simon chucked the paper back at him. "Cheeky sod!" He turned back to Nesta. "So, yeah, be careful what you throw out. It might be worth a fortune!"

"My Morgan used to call me a bit of a hoarder. I love a car boot sale. And a charity shop! Oh, the amount of charity shops in Mold — you know how hard it is to resist them?"

The bread stall owner chuckled. "I hear you. I'm terrible as well." He pointed towards Jake. "You know I used to try and persuade this one to keep the boxes for his toys growing up? Some of those *Action Men* would be worth a fortune now."

"Life's too short, dad!" Jake called out.

Simon folded up his arms. "As you can see — the lad still doesn't listen to me."

"There must be *something* you'd enjoy collecting," said Nesta, as the young man walked over with a disinterested face. "Everyone has something."

Jake huffed. "I like video games."

His father groaned. "You'll never make your money back on those things. Cost me a fortune!"

"Not true," said Jake. "You'd get thousands for an original *Mario* cartridge now. I saw it on a *Netflix* show."

Nesta understood very little of what the young man just said, but a sudden thought popped into her head. "Do you like *Call Of Duty*?"

Jake was stunned. "You know *Call Of Duty*?"

"Oh, yes." She couldn't help but look smug, especially with his father's confused stare. "I'm familiar with the old COD. I have a friend that plays regularly."

"Your friends play video games?"

"Don't look so surprised, young man. This friend would give you a run for your money."

Simon shook his head. "I can't be doing with all that violence and shooting. Like I said — there's enough of that in real life. It sounds like World War Three in our house with all that noise going off upstairs." The man paused and smirked in Nesta's direction. "You know what we did for this lad's birthday this year? Took him and his mates paintballing. What did they all do? Sat around in the woods and hid whilst playing on their phones. So much for *Call Of Customs* or whatever it's called. We'd be in real trouble if we *did* have to go to war."

Jake rolled his eyes. "It would be all drones, anyway, dad. I'd like to see you operating one of those."

"He's got me there," said Simon with a scoff.

"Speaking of guns," said Nesta, which is a sentence she never thought she would say. "Is there anyone else around here with an interest in collecting items designed to shoot people? Apart from Charlie?"

Simon removed his cap and began scratching his head. "Now you're asking," he said. "Charlie was very specific in the weaponry he collected. It wasn't just guns. As long as it had some historical significance, he was interested."

"Remember that sword he showed us?" asked Jake with an excited smile.

His father chuckled. "Yeah, you loved that one, didn't you? Can't believe he walked around with that thing in a carrier bag. It looked like something out of the Battle of Waterloo. Probably was, for all I know. But there's nobody that was as mad as he was. Except maybe Mel-Fruit-and-Veg."

Nesta needed no further elaboration on who *that* person might be. She likely sold fruit, and she likely sold veg. "That woman with the stall over in the square?"

Simon nodded. "I could see her being an arms dealer. Wouldn't want to mess with Mel. Her husband's a gamekeeper, and she was a national shooting champion."

"How interesting," said Nesta. "Sounds like she doesn't miss very often."

"I wouldn't want to be a pheasant, put it that way."

His customer nodded and handed over some money. "Keep the change," she said.

As Nesta turned around to walk away, her shoulder was barged by someone in a great hurry, causing her recent purchase to fall to the ground.

"Oh!" said the person responsible. "I'm so sorry!"

Nesta stared at her mangled Manchester tart with sorry eyes and looked up to see the face of Wendy Stephens.

"Let me help you," said Wendy, crouching down to retrieve the tart.

"It's fine," Nesta muttered.

"I do love a Manchester tart." Wendy studied the broken pastry and licked her finger with a wince. "A little dry for a tart, but I suppose that's what you get from a bread stall. I'll make sure to pass my feedback to Simon."

"Oh, I'm sure you will..."

Wendy clapped her hands in a burst of enthusiasm. "Are we ready for the next class? It's biscuit day!"

"I can't wait," said Nesta, as a hand was placed on her shoulder. She secretly had no intention of completing her course but would let her absence do the talking.

"I'm sure you'll be fine," said Wendy. "Follow my lead and nothing will go wrong. We all have to learn from our past mistakes. Don't stress. Things can only get better, eh?" She let out a high-pitched laugh. "Oh, and if you need any cakes or tarts next time, you know where to find me."

Nesta watched Wendy hurry off back to her cake stall and began to consider the idea of owning a firearm herself. You never knew when one might come in handy.

CHAPTER 14

Two figures sat in the corner of Daniel Owen Square, watching, listening and observing, as the crowd of shoppers swarmed around the market stalls like busy insects.

"It's not bad this," said Darren, munching away on his piece of pastry and custard.

Nesta sat beside him with the broken Manchester tart on her lap. She finished her own mouthful and frowned. "Not bad? It's got fruit, custard, pastry. What more do you want?"

Darren shrugged. "I'm not a big fan of cakes. I can take or leave them."

"Well, you can leave the rest of this tart well enough alone, then." She hugged the circular tray tight.

"You know that Dorothy woman didn't even buy anything after all that?" asked Darren with his mouthful. "You sure it's safe to leave her watching the stall?"

"She was sitting there on the bench anyway. We might as well have a break. Besides, we've got some surveillance work to do." Nesta gazed over at the fruit and vegetable stall over in the distance, specifically on the woman behind the counter.

Mel Searle had a physique that was more suited to lugging bails of hay than apples and oranges. She dwarfed her husband, Evan, by quite a margin and possessed hands that could quite easily crush his small skull like one of their coconuts.

"Is that her?" asked Darren. Nesta nodded. The teenager squinted at their target and shook his head. "Doesn't look like a champion shooter. The guy's tiny."

"Not the husband," said Nesta with a sigh. "The woman next to him."

"Oh," Darren muttered. "Yeah, she looks pretty crazy. But didn't you say Charlie had a load of guns too?"

"Yes, but he didn't shoot himself. Or the gun would have been lying next to him."

They both continued to follow the woman's movements, which involved packing up various bits of produce and exchanging them for handfuls of cash. Darren let out a long yawn and his attention became distracted by a pigeon wrestling with a slice of bread. "How long are we going to watch her for?"

Nesta had not moved a muscle and remained focused on the task in hand. "Until we see something suspicious."

The teenager checked his watch. "We could be here a while."

His companion groaned. "You'd make for a terrible stake-out. Aren't you enjoying the view?"

A confused Darren took another look at the busy square. "*What* view?"

"Don't you enjoy a little people-watching from time to time?" asked Nesta.

"You mean, stalking people? You're beginning to sound like that Dorothy woman who sits around on different benches."

Nesta spotted a toddler hobbling over to its mother nearby and smiled. "You young people just can't appreciate the simple pleasures in life. You're way too overstimulated. Take this sight right now. All the different people going about their own lives. We're all just ants moving around our colony."

Darren rolled his eyes. "Sounds like you need better glasses."

"Aren't you curious?" Nesta asked. She pointed towards two old men chatting outside the beauty salon. "Wouldn't you like to know what those two are talking about?"

"Probably their pensions."

Nesta shook her head. "I think people are fascinating. This is like our very own soap opera unfolding in real time."

Darren glanced down at the half-eaten Manchester tart on her lap and began to wonder if it was full of alcohol. "Doesn't beat a good action movie," he muttered.

"Have you ever seen a film called *The Conversation*?" Nesta asked. She received a blank stare.

"Who's in it?"

"It follows a surveillance expert played by Gene Hackman who listens in on this couple from a distance using a load of sound recording equipment. They're walking around a busy square much larger than this one."

"Doesn't sound as good as *The Fast and the Furious* movies," said Darren.

Nesta ignored him and pictured herself wearing similar head gear to Gene Hackman whilst listening in on the various conversations going on around her.

Darren stretched out his arms and yawned again. "So what was so special about this conversation anyway?"

The woman beside him smiled. "It involved a potential murder." She could feel the teenager sitting up and leaning forward. *Now* he was interested, she thought.

"What were they talking about?" Darren asked.

"Oh, so *now* you're interested? I guess people aren't as boring as you think. You'll have to just watch the film for yourself."

The young man folded up his arms with a grunt. "There's no way I'm sitting through a whole black and white movie just to find that out. Life's too short."

Nesta was just about to point out that *The Conversation* was actually in full technicolour, when she spotted a familiar face heading towards the fruit and vegetable stall.

Jason Potts was dressed in the same hi-vis coat that she had seen him wear at the back of the church. The groundskeeper bypassed the selection of wholesome produce and made a B-line for the woman standing behind the counter.

"That's him," Nesta whispered.

"I don't know why you're whispering," said Darren. "There's no way they'll hear you from all the way over there."

She hushed him regardless, and they both watched Jason hand Mel a handful of notes.

"He's just handed her some money!" Nesta cried.

Darren saw the woman pocket the cash. "Maybe he just wants to buy some bananas?"

Nesta shook her head and studied the man's pale complexion. "There's no way that man's getting his five a day."

"Hey," said Darren. "Do you think that guy's a hitman? Maybe she paid him to shoot Charlie!"

This time, it was Nesta's turn to be cynical. "You think he'd still be cutting grass if he was a contract killer?"

"Could be undercover."

"Then why is he giving *her* money?"

Darren nodded. "I know what you're thinking. The fruit and veg woman is the assassin!"

Nesta didn't even acknowledge his theory with a response. "I wish I knew what they were saying." She turned to look at Darren's mobile phone and was struck by an epiphany. "Does that thing record sound?"

The teenager looked at her with horrified eyes. "No way. You're not using my phone to do that."

Moments later, Nesta was making her way across the square towards Mel's stall. She moved in her most casual manner possible, browsing the various fruits and vegetables like any other curious punter. Darren looked on, helplessly, from the other side of the square, cringing, as his partner in crime stood out like a sore thumb.

Nesta inspected a box full of avocados, as she worked her way closer towards the conversation happening only a few yards away. In one fluid movement, she pulled out the mobile phone from her pocket and placed it in between a line of melons. Like a victorious bank robber, she made a swift escape with an excited smile across her face.

"I did it!" she cried when returning back to a weary Darren. "I feel just like Gene Hackman!"

"Could you be anymore obvious?" Darren hissed. "Next time, let *me* do the planting."

Nesta sat back down beside him and scoffed. "I've done more planting in my life than you have, young man. When was the last time you grew a load of tomatoes?"

The perplexed teenager shook his head and turned his attention back to their target. Mel and Jason were still chatting away, and an excited Nesta rubbed her hands.

"Now we just sit back and wait," she said.

Once the groundsworker had bid his farewells and walked away, Nesta made the return journey back to the stall to retrieve her device. When she arrived at the melons, her face dropped.

"Looking for this?" asked Mel.

Nesta turned around and saw the woman clutching Darren's mobile phone with a disapproving frown.

"Oh!" Nesta cried. "Thank goodness you've found it! I must have dropped it."

A highly suspicious Mel handed it back to her. "I know you've been watching me," the woman said. "I spotted you twenty minutes ago. You and your little friend."

They both turned to see a guilty-looking Darren over on the other side of the square trying to avoid eye contact.

Nesta went a bright shade of red. "Oh, *him*? He's not my friend. He's my... grandson."

Mel's eyebrow was now half way up her forehead. "Who are you? Mmh?" Mel glared at the older woman with piercing eyes that would make a criminal fold under questioning. "Police? Press?" She groaned. "God, you're not one of those anti-hunting maniacs, are you? I've had enough of those."

Nesta chose her next words very carefully. "I'm none of those things, I can assure you." She racked her brains. "You might say that I'm something of a private investigator."

Mel stared at her serious expression and howled with laughter. "A private detective? In Mold? Now I've heard everything." She shook her head and began laying out a new box of potatoes.

"I'm investigating the murder of a friend of mine," Nesta added. There was no response. "His name was Charlie Coogan."

The woman let go of her potatoes and turned around. "Old Charlie?"

"You knew him?"

Mel let out a grunt and carried on with her work. "I knew him a little. I quite liked the bloke, actually. We had a similar outlook on the world. Anyone who goes off to war for their own country deserves my respect."

"Did you see him often?"

"Down the market obviously," said Mel. "He came round my house once to buy an old rifle. That's when we properly hit it off."

Nesta nodded. "Charlie was something of a collector."

"Yes," said Mel with a slightly judgmental tone in her voice. "That's where we differed. I never understood his obsession with collecting old junk. He paid me a decent amount for that rifle. The damn thing probably doesn't even work! I'm a bit more practical. But, still, we had other things in common."

"Like what?"

Mel put down her boxes and stood tall. "Backbone." She turned to her husband, who was busy unloading some carrots. "If my Evan was half the man Charlie was, I'd be a lucky woman. Isn't that right, Evan?" The timid man failed to hear her call. "Useless, he is."

"Charlie struck me as quite a gentle soul," said Nesta.

Mel laughed. "Gentle? Try putting a twelve-bore in his hands and call him gentle. The man was a trained killer. And a bloody good shot! I invited him to one of our hunts."

"Hunts?"

"Well, I say hunts. Shooting down pheasants is hardly proper hunting. But good target practice."

"Ah, yes." Nesta smiled. "I heard you were a shooting champion."

Mel squinted her eyes to study this strange pensioner. She was good. Very good. Perhaps, the fruit and vegetable trader had underestimated her. Luckily, she was quite happy to dismiss her suspicions when it came to a compliment. "I was the best in the country," she said. "Charlie could shoot, but he was no match for yours truly." The woman smirked as a pleasant thought entered her head. "I would have made a damn good soldier, too, come to think of it. The army could have done with my skills." She began visualising herself in the lead role of her favourite war films: *Apocalypse Now*, *Platoon*, *Full Metal Jacket* — even *Commando*. Schwarzenegger could eat his heart out, she thought.

Nesta allowed for the long pause, as it appeared that the other woman was in her own world.

"You mentioned anti-hunting people earlier," she said, eventually.

The mere reminder was enough to make the passionate hunter groan. "Parasites, the lot of them." She glanced over at someone heading past and shuddered. "There's one now."

Nesta looked over to see Claire waving at her. "The coffee girl?"

Mel scoffed. "I wouldn't drink her coffee if you paid me. She'd likely poison me."

"Oh, surely not." They watched the young woman with purple hair crouch down to stroke a cheerful Labrador. "She seems nice enough to me."

"Don't be fooled," Mel snapped, scrunching up her nose. "That girl once drew skulls and crossbones all over my pumpkins. I know it was her. She knows full well what I do in my spare time."

"The game keeping?" asked Nesta. "I doubt she would have a problem with that. I grew up on a farm myself, you see. People need to eat."

The mention of Nesta's farming background caused Mel to lower her guard. "I'm not talking about the pheasants," Mel said. "That's child's play. I've hunted bigger animals than that."

"You mean, like deer hunting?"

"Among other things." Mel smiled. "That's probably as exciting as you can get in this country. You need to go abroad for the real fun." She pulled out her phone and showed off a series of photographs. Nesta wanted to look away, as she was succumbed to images of dead animals. Farming was one thing, but she could never fathom the idea of hunting for sport.

"Elk is my favourite," said Mel. "Have you ever eaten elk?"

"Can't say I have," Nesta muttered, trying to shake the images out of her head."

"You've not lived until you've hunted down your own prey

and eaten it that night." Mel's excitement appeared to be overwhelming her, as if she was about to leap forward and eat Nesta whole. "Very nutritious, too. I brought back a load from America and stuck it in my freezer. They say you inherit the animal's soul — and I believe it! You can literally feel its strength inside of you afterwards. It makes you feel invincible, like you have the strength of a wild predator."

Nesta watched her crush the mango in her hand and swallowed a hard gulp. "Sounds lovely."

Mel nodded. "You never forget your first kill." The woman rubbed her hands together. "I can't wait to head back out there for the next season." She gave a cheeky grin and glanced over at her unsuspecting husband. "Don't tell my other half, but I've already started planning my dream trip."

Nesta hoped that she was talking about a nice cruise somewhere but was soon to be disappointed. She watched the woman grab a rolled-up magazine which appeared to be falling apart from overuse.

"Take a look at this," Mel continued, presenting her with a page that included the heading: *African Hunting Holiday*.

Nesta felt her blood run cold. She had heard of such holidays but seeing one advertised like a resort getaway to Majorca made it even more disturbing.

Mel could see the older woman's discomfort and it fuelled her excitement. Not everyone was cut out to hunt down a lion in the wild, and she loved the idea of being a one-of-a-kind. "Some people find it barbaric. But that doesn't make them right. We're the most dominant species on the planet, and we deserve our right to exercise that. We were born to hunt. It's survival of the fittest." Her happy grin remained, and she pulled out her mobile phone. "I know I'm not the only one who thinks this. Thank God for the internet."

Nesta peered at the small screen, as the woman scrolled

down a feed of social media posts with hundreds of likes and comments. "You have a lot of followers," she said.

Mel tilted her head up with pride. "Post good content and they'll come. There's a lot of smart, like-minded people out there."

"I actually have a following of my own," said Nesta. She looked away from the graphic posts.

"You?" asked Mel, who did not appreciate having her thunder stolen. She had never expected this curious pensioner to know the first thing about social media and assumed that she must have been mistaken.

Nesta gave a smug jiggle. "I'm a regular feature on my friend's true crime channel. One of my videos went viral." She thought about her moment down by Bala's lake, when Darren had introduced her to the wonders of online filmmaking.

Mel snarled her lip and put her phone away. "Yes, well. People will watch anything these days."

Nesta turned to see Darren over in the distance feeding a pigeon with a piece of her tart. "Our case over in Bala was quite different to Charlie's. There were no guns involved for a start. This could have been anyone."

"What makes you think that?" asked Mel, turning back to deal with her potatoes.

"Well," said Nesta. "Anyone can pull a trigger."

Her words caused the other woman's broad shoulders to tighten. "Whoever killed Charlie knew what they were doing. People have no idea how difficult it is to shoot someone. All those cowboy films have made it look easy. But you try lifting up a handgun and blowing someone away with one shot. It just isn't realistic."

"You speak as if you've tried to do it."

Mel's large head snapped around to look at her mischievous smile. She wasn't the least bit amused. "I've shot enough moving animals in my time to know how hard it is. Just because you have the tool doesn't mean you can do the job."

Shame the animals can't shoot back, Nesta thought. She began to worry about the pigeon nibbling on her tart. It wasn't safe with Mel Searle around.

"We humans have been taking aim at things since we invented the spear," Mel continued. "Not that much has changed. Spear, bow, gun — you still need the same level of nerve and composure — to strike at the right moment. Like a snake or a tiger. It all happens in a split second. We're an a-pex predator."

Nesta watched the passionate hunter act out the movement of a cobra with her large forearm, snapping her hand like a pair of fangs. She wanted to slowly back away until she was safely out of range. It appeared that Mel didn't normally get to discuss her hobby with many people, and Nesta could see why.

"You know," said Mel. "I'm looking at taking up bow hunting."

It didn't surprise Nesta, but she feigned a sense of surprise. "Are you really? How interesting. I've just taken up baking again."

Mel was good at detecting fear and presence but sarcasm didn't seem to be on her radar. "Bow hunting is how you *really* get back to our roots. You can really become one with nature again."

As long as she wasn't killing most of it, Nesta thought.

"It takes pure skill and dedication to take down an elk with a bow and arrow. There's no mistakes. You only get one chance."

"As long as it's just the elks," said Nesta with a nervous laugh.

"The ultimate predator," said Mel, mimicking herself taking aim and pulling back a draw string.

"Where do you want these cabbages, love?"

Mel turned to her husband and wanted to scold him for interrupting.

"Right," said Nesta, checking her watch. "I better get going." She began walking away, when Mel reminded her of Darren's phone.

"I wouldn't worry about the audio recording, by the way." Mel jiggled the mobile in her hand. "I stopped it recording as soon as you first left it."

An embarrassed Nesta took the phone back and made the long walk of shame back across the square.

Darren was waiting for her with an eager face. "Well? How did it go? You reckon she's a suspect?"

Nesta slumped herself down beside him. "Oh, she's a killer, alright. In more ways than one."

CHAPTER 15

Mold market was at the end of another Saturday, and its stalls were now literally shells of their former selves. Their hollow, steel frames were gradually being dismantled, and the hustle and bustle of the high street had died down into a deserted space for vans and trailers.

Nesta and Darren made their way down the street to the sound of clanking steel and high-pitched conversations between fellow tired traders. There was a certain sadness to the sight of these stripped-down market stalls, like a discarded Christmas tree on a cold January morning.

Nesta sighed. "Well, there we are. Another market day done and dusted. Another day, another dollar."

"Or fifty-pence in our case," Darren muttered.

"Now, now. None of this negativity. We made ten pounds today. That's a new record."

Darren huffed. "It's pretty easy to break a record when your last result was nothing."

Nesta gave him a nudge. "That's a hundred percent increase."

"A hundred percent increase of zero is zero."

"Yes, alright. You know what I mean. Your maths is better than mine, so I'll take your word for it. The point is — we're improving every time. Next time, we'll make a fortune!"

"Great. I'll start booking my holiday." Darren looked around at all the vans being loaded up around him. "How do you reckon these guys did?"

"Maybe we should ask someone." Nesta turned to the nearest person she could find, who happened to be a woman that sold dream catchers. "Good result today?"

Millie Hogan stood up in her long, colourful dress. "I sold a couple of wind chimes," she said. "And a load of herbal products. They're usually my bread and butter."

Nesta shook her head. "It's not easy." She studied the woman's broad mix of products, which included everything from greeting cards to some mysterious books on the occult. It was hard not to be impressed. Surely, she thought, if someone could sell a range of items *this* obscure, then it should have been no trouble selling her knitting. "What's your secret?" she asked. "How do you get more sales?"

Millie smiled. "Human beings are emotional creatures. Half of what we buy we don't need. We're just always searching for more. People buy on instinct. They also buy into the person that's selling. When you buy one of my products, you buy a piece of me."

The woman spoke as though she was an otherworldly spirit, and Nesta would not have been surprised if Millie had just floated away before her very eyes. "What are those?" she asked, pointing at a row of bronze nuggets.

"They're whatever you want them to be," said Millie. "If you keep one in your pocket, they can bring you good luck."

Nesta reached into her handbag. "I'll take two of them," she said.

Darren shook his head in disgust, as they both continued their stroll down the high street. "She played you like a fiddle," he said.

"Whatever do you mean?"

"The woman just told you that people buy stuff they don't need. Then she sold you some pieces of metal."

"Don't be so cynical," said Nesta. "We need all the luck we can get." She stopped walking and froze. "Look!"

They both saw Jason Potts, standing outside a betting shop on the other side of the road. The grounds worker was hard to miss in his bright, yellow jacket, and he blew out a final lungful of cigarette smoke into the air before heading inside the nearest pub.

Nesta turned to Darren with an excited grin. "Looks like our luck really is changing."

Before the teenager could reply, she was already leading him inside a pub called *The Silver Heron*. The atmosphere was quite lively for that time of day, and cheap pints of lager were flowing throughout the room.

Having walked in from the bright sunlight outside, Nesta was struggling to adjust her eyes and find who she was looking for. Darren followed her across a carpeted floor, which was dark enough to hide the endless stains of spilt wine and beer.

"There he is," Nesta whispered and pulled the teenager into their own private booth.

Jason Potts was on his own table less than a roasted peanut throw away, immersed in a giant newspaper that covered up his face.

"Do we really need to do another stake-out?" asked Darren.

"Steak!" Nesta cried, sliding him a menu. "Great idea. Best to try and look like a normal customer."

"I wouldn't say *normal* is ever the right word with you," Darren muttered. His low mood was altered by the list of hearty dishes on offer. Fortunately, he was very hungry. "So what's your plan now? Hope it's better than the last one."

Nesta threw a napkin at him and tried to think. She hadn't actually thought her next move through. "We need to find out why he was talking to Mel. Apart from me, there were only two other people present in that graveyard after Charlie was shot, and he was one of them."

Jason continued to browse his newspaper and sip on his pint, oblivious to the fact he was being watched from afar. Suddenly, the man was joined by another person that Nesta recognised.

"It's him," she whispered from the safety of her booth.

Darren squinted at the burly looking second man with jet-black hair and a *Liverpool F.C.* shirt. "I've never seen that other guy before in my life."

Nesta sighed. "Were you paying no attention whatsoever in that square? He was another man who approached that fruit and veg woman — about five minutes before Jason did. Remember?" The teenager gave her a blank stare, and she groaned. "Honestly, you young people have the attention span of a ferret. Good job you're not on any surveillance team."

Her words had already fallen on deaf ears, as Darren was more preoccupied with his menu. "What do you reckon? Scampi or chicken nuggets? I'm thinking both."

Nesta ignored him and turned around to observe the two men. "It's a shame that Jason fellow is not alone. I was hoping to speak with him." She continued to watch, until both Jason and his large associate folded up their newspapers and left their table. "Wait here! I'll be right back. Order me a cod and chips." She placed a twenty pound note on the table, which was more than enough to satisfy the teenager, and leapt up to follow the two men towards the main doors, hoping they were heading out for a cigarette.

Jason and his Liverpool fan exited the pub with bleary eyes

and strolled across the main road without a care or worry in the world. Little did they know it then, but the two men had a determined Nesta Griffiths in hot pursuit. After both of them had abruptly parted ways, Jason headed straight inside the local betting shop, a place that the woman behind him had never frequented in her life.

There was a first time for everything (Nesta had discovered as of late), and she entered the local bookies with a mixed feeling of excitement and apprehension. "Look natural," she told herself, strutting her way through a room circled with monitors. Regular punters were all loitering in their various corners, staring up at the screens with gormless expressions. A few of them, Nesta had noticed, had barely seen the light of day, and she made her way to the counter in the hope of appearing like she participated in this activity every day.

"Good afternoon," she said to the woman behind her large desk. "I'm looking to place a bet, please."

The cashier lowered her glasses and seemed annoyed to be distracted from her magazine. "You might need to be more specific."

"Oh," said Nesta, gazing around at the colourful advertisements nearby. "What's the next horse race?"

"Seventeen-fifty-eight at Hexham."

"I'll take that one."

The woman behind the desk sighed. "You'll need a horse."

"Ah! Of course." Nesta was handed a list of options, and her eyes scanned through the quirky names. One name in particular jumped out at her, and it was almost as if the decision had been made for her. "Morgan's Dream, please."

The cashier raised her eyebrow. "You've seen the odds on that one?"

Nesta nodded with a grin. "This is one of those gut feelings."

She walked off with her betting slip in hand and headed over to join the hopefuls standing around the room.

Jason Potts was buried in his newspaper when she approached, and he hadn't even sensed her presence beside him.

"I know you," Nesta said, as though their encounter was pure chance. "You're that man I saw outside the church."

Jason looked up from his treasured sporting columns and seemed annoyed to be disturbed. He gave the woman a confused stare.

"The day Charlie Coogan died? I was the woman with the dogs?"

"Oh," said Jason with a nod. "I remember."

Nesta stood beside him, looking up at the wall of monitors. "Let's hope we're luckier than he was that day, eh?"

Jason glanced down at the slip in her hand. "Morgan's Dream? You know what the odds are on that one?" The woman's nod made him curious. "You know something I don't?"

"Sometimes you just get a feeling," said Nesta.

Jason chuckled. "I've had many of them. I'm still skint, though." He folded up his newspaper and sighed. "Aye, it's a shame about that Charlie, bloke. He was alright. Bought a load of fishing gear from him down the market once."

"Did you see anything suspicious on the day he was shot?" Nesta asked.

"Not really. I was cutting the grass when the gun went off. I thought it was a car backfiring or something, especially with the lawnmower running."

"How could you tell where it came from?"

"I couldn't. Not until I headed round the building to find you and the vicar. I was down at the opposite side of the yard."

"Then what made you come around the building if you thought it was just a car backfiring?"

Jason glared at her. Her argumental tone surprised him. "Just being cautious, I suppose. It was my first day on the job."

Nesta saw his suspicious stare and decided to go easy on the questioning. "Fair enough. That must have been quite the first day. Not everyone has to face a murder investigation when they start a new job."

"Tell me about it," Jason muttered. "It was a nightmare. Once the police were called, I couldn't even finish. I thought the agency were going to go mental."

"So you do temping?"

Jason folded up his arms in a sulk. "Never used to. I had a permanent job for over ten years at a factory near Shotton. Skilled work it was. You had to be trained up for a couple of years on the job as an apprentice. The only trouble was those skills weren't transferable to anything else, and we all got made redundant after the company went bust. Me and a load of others."

"What were you making at this factory?"

"Batteries," Jason muttered.

Nesta couldn't help but feel sorry for the man. Fortunately, her teaching job at Bala Secondary School had been a job for life, and she couldn't imagine being told that she suddenly had to find another school. "I'm sorry to hear that."

Jason sighed. "Yeah, well. Nothing's guaranteed. But bills are. Now the kids want to go to *Legoland* this year." He pointed towards the monitors. "That's why I'm hoping for a bit of luck."

They both stared at the hypnotic colours of a football match taking place on a nearby screen. "I don't know an awful lot about gambling." Nesta smiled at the thought of a recent memory. "Although, I recently did okay on a slot machine over in Talacre." She turned to see that the man had opened up his newspaper again and was scanning a list of fixtures. "But I know enough to realise that the odds are stacked in the bookies' favour."

"Not always," said Jason, circling some columns with his pen. "Knowledge is power in this game. That's why I focus my betting on football."

Nesta spotted the tattoo on the man's forearm and recognised the logo. "You a Wrexham fan?"

The man's face lit up. "Since the day I was born. My old man was a fanatic like me." He thought about the recent investment of a certain film star and his deep pockets. "We're finally getting what we deserve after all these years of pain and suffering."

"Can you really know enough about football to beat the odds?" Nesta asked. She saw the miserable faces on the people around them and found it hard not to be cynical.

"Course," said Jason. "My wife reckons I should have been a football manager with my knowledge. I used to tape matches and study all the players. I still collect all the *Premier League* player cards. Been doing that since I was a kid." His face darkened. "Can't afford to do that this year. Those things aren't cheap."

"You know Charlie Coogan was a bit of a collector?"

Jason nodded. "I got that impression. We chatted a bit about collectibles when I bought that fishing gear off him. There's big money in card collections. He was going to value a few of mine but we never got round to it."

Nesta gazed down at her betting slip and checked her watch. Her race was imminent, and the anticipation was killing her. "I was going to say hello to you earlier," she said. "I saw you over at Mel's fruit and veg stall."

Jason smirked. "She's a right character, isn't she?"

"I get the impression that she sells more than just plant-based products," said Nesta, waiting for a reaction.

"She's definitely got her fingers in a lot of pies," said Jason.

The man took a quick scan of the room and lowered his voice. "Me and a few of the guys have some shares in a little project of hers."

Nesta saw the mischief in his eyes and was ready to hear more. "Go on."

"Well, she's got this greyhound..."

His last word sparked a wave of both confusion and slight disappointment within his listener. "A greyhound?"

Jason nodded. "A little syndicate, if you like. His name's Destiny's Hound."

"Wait a minute." Nesta took a moment to make sure that she wasn't losing her mind. "Are you telling me that this woman is a dog breeder? And you're paying her money towards it?" She saw him nodding with pride. "Didn't you say that money was tight?"

The grounds worker shook his head and began searching his pockets. "Nah, nah. This dog is different. He's going to make us all a fortune."

Nesta rolled her eyes and watched him pull out a piece of folded-up paper. "You should see the dog's pedigree." He unfolded the document as though it were a treasure map. "Check out the bloodline on this lad."

They both gathered around a family tree full of various dog names. "You see," said Jason. "Destiny goes all the way back to Doggy Galore." He waited for the gasp and instead received a blank stare. "The famous racing hound? He won more races than I can remember. Imagine having that blood racing through your veins."

Nesta began staring at the pedigree tree but could no longer see canine names. The entire image ignited a sudden thought in her head. "Family tree... yes, that's what he was looking through."

It was now Jason's turn to look confused. "Hey?"

"Oh, it's just something the vicar said. It can wait."

The mention of his temporary employer made Jason go cold. "Don't get me started on that bloke. He's a real taskmaster."

Nesta gave an understanding nod and pointed upwards towards the heavens. "So is the vicar's boss, I imagine." She took one final glance at the pedigree chart before it was put away. "I can't believe that woman managed to convince a load of people to give her money towards a greyhound. She creates life as well as taking it away." She glanced back up at the ceiling. "A bit like someone else I know."

"We pay her every month," said Jason. "We all have equal shares in that dog. We've been there since he was born. Mel's very good at what she does." He rubbed his hands together. "He'll be ready for his first race soon. I'll get to sit in the owner's box." Jason raised up his chin and jiggled his head.

"Oh!" Nesta pointed towards the screen up ahead. "My race is starting!" She clutched her betting slip tight, as the line of horses burst into action. Morgan's Dream had got off to a good start and began leading the charge with his brightly-coloured jockey. "Go on! Go on, Morgan's Dream!"

Nesta's cries were enough to attract the attention of other punters and a couple of them headed over to join her. Even Jason had placed his newspaper down and was surprised by the early lead. "I said it before," he announced to the rest of the room, pointing at the excited newbie. "This woman knows something we don't!"

Soon, the entire betting shop was chanting away alongside her, as Morgan's Dream maintained his steady pace around the track. The horse approached the finish line with the confidence of a champion, only to have his victory ruined by two other contenders.

"No!" Nesta cried. "No! That's not fair!" Her eyes closed, as Morgan's Dream's stamina had failed him once again.

The row of onlookers all sniggered and departed back to

their usual corners of the room. Nesta scrunched up her betting slip and threw it towards the screen like a regular.

"Told you the odds were rubbish," Jason muttered. "Now you know why. Should have gone with Baby Boomer."

The woman beside him resisted the urge to bite his head off and left the betting shop for what would be the very last time. Perhaps her "sign" had been Morgan's way of teaching her a lesson for putting money on an animal she had never met. Or maybe it had been one of his childish practical jokes. That would have been just like him, Nesta thought to herself. She looked up at the sky with a disapproving frown. "I hope you're pleased with yourself. You just cost me a tenner!"

CHAPTER 16

"You need to hit enter," Darren snapped. His patience was already quite low after spending half an hour waiting for Nesta to acquire the password for her daughter's computer. Erin was not an easy person to get hold of, and acquiring any type of administrational information from *her* was harder than getting water out of a cactus. Fortunately, Nesta was like a high-pressured drinking straw, and she soon had everything they needed. She had even managed to get the login details of her son's *Lineage* account, something he had been paying the subscription to for over a year (but, like many subscriptions, still hadn't quite got around to making use of it).

The genealogy website had grown from strength to strength over the last decade and allowed its users to access a wealth of family history that anyone could add to or update.

Nesta already knew that Charlie Coogan had been a big fan of the platform, and the sight of Jason Potts' pedigree chart had inspired her to delve into the Coogan family tree. But, first, she had to navigate the treacherous waters of the internet which had been no easy feat with someone shouting in her ear.

"No, you have to put the whole address in," said Darren, rubbing his tired face.

"I know, I know." Nesta bashed at the keyboard. "Believe it or not, I have actually operated one of these things before."

"Operated?" Darren shook his head. He knew he should have insisted on taking the wheel, as his driver was doomed to crash.

"There," she said. "Now what do we do?"

They both stared at the computer screen, which featured a flashing search field.

"You search for Charlie Coogan," said Darren.

A few taps later, and they were soon staring at the man's profile.

"It hasn't yet registered his death," said Nesta. She felt the same chill that always happened when receiving a letter addressed to her husband. It never seemed to get easier.

"I guess someone would need to update it." The teenager pointed to an icon at the top of Charlie's name. "Click that."

Nesta clicked her mouse and a chain of other names populated the screen.

"Looks like Charlie's been busy," said Darren, scanning the profiles of the man's relatives. "The tree keeps going." He grabbed hold of the mouse and began scrolling upwards to reveal more names.

"How far does this go back?" asked Nesta. She saw one date of birth in particular. "This one was born during the reign of Queen Victoria."

Darren continued to scroll. "I think you can keep adding as much info as you like."

"Wait, go back." Nesta pointed downwards. "There was a name — just — there! I knew I recognised it."

They both stared at the profile of an Edward Delyn.

"That was the name on one of the gravestones," said Darren.

Nesta smiled and patted him on the back. "So you *do* pay attention."

The teenager ignored her comment and frowned. "But Charlie's surname was Coogan. And, yet, most of his ancestors were Delyn."

"His mother married a Coogan." Nesta pointed at one of the profiles above Charlie's name. She began scrolling back up again. "But he definitely seemed more interested in his Delyn side of the family. It just keeps going."

"Look!" Darren cried. The mouse froze, and he pointed at a name from the eighteenth century. "They're all Lords and Ladies."

He wasn't wrong, Nesta thought. The names that preceded Charlie's were littered with titles. "Well," she said. "That explains the inheritance. And the big house on Clwydian Road."

"Shouldn't he be living in some kind of mansion or something?" Darren asked. "With servants and stuff?"

Nesta didn't answer his question and began filling the short silence with gentle murmurs. "Charlie, Charlie... what a past you have." She eventually turned off her daughter's computer and rubbed her eyes. Those screens had always played havoc on her vision.

"So what does all this mean?"

Nesta shook her head. "I have no idea. This man was complicated enough already. Now he's an aristocrat who became a soldier. Then, a soldier who became a market trader."

"You think someone killed him for his money?"

"He didn't seem to have very much," said Nesta. "Apart from the house obviously. Why else would he still be working if he had enormous wealth?"

Darren shrugged. "Some people like working. I know my

dad does." His sad expression had not gone unnoticed, and the woman behind the computer desk nodded.

"True. I suppose money isn't everything. I should know, being retired. Sometimes you need something to occupy your time."

Taylor and Kim were snoozing on a nearby sofa, as Hari had to make do with the carpet. He had given up trying to find a common ground with these two cockapoos. Besides, there were two of them and one of him.

Darren had expected to be on the couch himself that night but had been pleased to hear about the spare room. The clock tower of St Mary's Church was a key feature in the view outside his window, and it was hard not to be reminded of the event that had taken place outside.

"How big was this house of his?" Darren asked, as they stepped outside into the back garden.

Nesta turned to him and smiled. "How about we find out."

~

Clwydian Road was as quiet as Nesta had expected on a Saturday night in Mold. The residents of this street were either out and about or tucked up inside for the night. Even at such a late hour, the sun had yet to fully set, and she made her way past a series of modest bungalows.

"How long is this street?" asked Darren, eventually. He gazed down at his mobile phone and studied his satellite map.

Nesta rolled her eyes. "How about you take in the real thing instead of staring down at that square full of pixels?"

Darren ignored her advice and began zooming out on his online map. Clwydian Road had been the other side of town and seemed to snake around on elevated ground. The further they walked, the larger the houses seemed to get.

Eventually, they reached the opening to a small park with an open gate.

On the opposite side of the street was an enormous house which seemed to rise up above everything else in sight. This Georgian property appeared very out of place, like a black sheep that nobody wanted to visit. Its driveway was larger than most of the other back gardens, and a row of tall hedges served their purpose of keeping out unwanted passersby. The building itself was in dire need of some overdue maintenance work, as its roof appeared to be missing more than a few tiles.

"The Addams Family springs to mind," said Darren.

Nesta stood beside him, nodding, as they faced the uninviting entrance.

"It's not exactly warm and cosy," she said, crossing the street to get a better look. Darren followed with a slight hesitation. The very sight of the house's murky windows gave him the creeps, and he imagined being greeted at the front door by a giant man with a square head and bolts through his neck.

"I don't know what you think we're going to find here," Darren whispered. "We know there's nobody home."

Nesta studied the surrounding neighbourhood before turning her attention back to the looming building. "We have to allow ourselves the opportunity for clues. You never know what you might find."

Darren folded up his arms and huffed. "It would help if this was actually the murderer's house. But Charlie lived alone. So there was no killer wife or lodger."

"As far as we know," said Nesta. She crossed the driveway and headed towards one of the sash windows.

"Great," Darren muttered to himself. "So now we're trespassing." He let out a sigh and lifted up his phone. "Oh, well. Guess I might as well get some footage."

Nesta was peering through one of the panes of glass when

the teenager approached, and she could see him filming in the dark reflection. "Probably not a good idea to film us walking around the property of a recent murder victim."

Darren didn't appear to be fazed and merely shrugged. "The house comes out great on camera. I could add some creepy music to the video."

"There's nobody home."

Nesta and Darren both jumped. The third voice had come from behind, and they turned around to find an elderly woman with a Beagle.

"I'm Gemma," she said, pointing to the house on the other side of the wall. "I live next door."

Nesta gave her teenage associate an awkward look and tried to think on her feet. "Oh, we're aware of the owner's situation," she said.

Gemma stared at her with a confused face. "Situation? You mean — he's dead..."

There was a short silence.

"Uh, yes." Nesta scratched her head. "That's basically what I meant. We're investigating the man's suspicious death."

"His murder?"

"Yes."

Gemma's face lit up. "How exciting! Are you private detectives?"

"You could say that we're private investigators," said Nesta, who could see Darren's surprise in the corner of her eye. "We'd just like to get to the bottom of what happened."

"Wouldn't we all," said Gemma, looking up at the large house. "I can only imagine the skeletons up in those closets."

"What do you mean?" asked Nesta.

"Well, Charlie was quite an unusual neighbour. A good neighbour, nonetheless."

"You got along well with him?"

Gemma nodded. "He cared a lot about his community. Even though he was only here about five years."

"I heard that he had some unusual views on crime prevention," said Nesta, thinking back to her conversation with Samir."

"Ah, yes." Gemma chuckled. "He certainly liked to take the law into his own hands." She pointed her walking stick towards the gate on the other side of the road. "We used to have terrible trouble with people hanging around outside that park." She lowered her voice. "You know, the type of people who were always up to no good?"

Nesta gazed over at what was a walled park with a sign that read: Clogwyn Gardens. "But they don't hang around anymore?"

Gemma shook her head. "That was all thanks to Charlie. He had a real way with people."

"How did you know they were up to no good?" Darren asked with a slightly defensive tone. He was no stranger to hanging around public areas himself when trying to pass the time. "It's a free country."

His remarks caused the woman's face to sour. "Not when you start chucking stones at innocent people's homes." She scrunched up her nose. "That's how it all started. They had the option of leaving us alone, but they decided to pick a fight."

"Us?" asked Nesta. She began to wonder how much of these words were her own and not her militant neighbour's.

"The residents of this street," said Gemma. "I always knew those people across the road were breaking the law, but I could never prove it. I used to watch them going in and out of that park from my bedroom window. Sometimes I'd take Reggie in there for a stroll." She pointed down at the Beagle. "I found a load of them looking very guilty when they saw me one night. They were clearly doing something illegal, and I told them all to go home or I'd call the police. This caused them to hurl abuse at me until I reached the park entrance. Poor Reggie was petrified."

"What a horrible bunch," said Nesta. "They're lucky I wasn't there. Or I'd have given them a right earful."

"She really would have, too," said Darren. "What happened next?"

"That's when we were approached by Charlie," said Gemma. She had a twinkle in her eye that suggested this was going to be her favourite part of the story. "He was holding a walking stick, which I hadn't seen on him before. The man seemed to walk just fine without help. He began threatening the group to back off. They seemed to find his behaviour quite amusing, and then turned their abuse on him. That's when he surprised everyone."

Darren was hanging on her every word. "Well? What did he do?" He imagined the older man revealing himself to be a martial arts master, twirling his cane around and taking the entire gang down single-handedly.

"He took the handle of his walking stick," said Gemma, "and pulled it away to reveal an enormous blade."

"A blade?" Nesta asked in shock.

"It was the length of the cane," Gemma continued. "Like a fencing sword. The walking stick turned out to be a long sheath concealing it. I'd not seen anything like it. It was very James Bond."

"He must have scared the living daylights out of that rowdy group," said Nesta.

Gemma laughed. "Oh, you better believe it! I think they all thought he was mad and not afraid to use it. They scarpered pretty quickly."

"Sounds awesome," said Darren.

Nesta gave the excited teenager a disapproving frown. "I can see what you mean about his tendency to take the law into his own hands," she said.

The elderly neighbour sighed. "Yep. He was a real trooper. I'll miss that man."

"I can't say that I exactly condone his methods," Nesta said.

"But they were effective," Gemma snapped. "Someone had to do something. It's easy to judge when these problems aren't on your very own doorstep. We need more people like Charlie around."

Nesta could see that the woman felt very strongly about what she was talking about. Her friendly demeanour had quickly slipped into an angry one. "Did you ever see him use any guns?"

Gemma's frown melted away. "Oh, no. Nothing like that. Although, I know he owned a few. He was a bit of a collector. The man once showed me his collection of knives. Now *that* was a sight to behold."

"Where did he keep all of those?" Darren asked, trying not to sound too enthusiastic.

"The knives were all in the attic, along with the swords." Her mention of the swords only fueled the teenager's interest even further. "But the guns were all in the shed."

"His garden shed?" Nesta asked. "He kept a load of firearms in a garden shed?"

"Garden shed is probably an understatement," said Gemma. "We're talking about more of a log cabin, really. It was apparently his sanctuary."

"Like a man cave?" asked Darren. Nesta rolled her eyes.

"Yes, I suppose it was something like that. He kept a lot of his little military keepsakes, photos, that sort of thing."

Nesta stared at the large house, wishing she possessed some x-ray vision to get a better look of the back garden. If it was like everything else on this property, it was likely to be sizable. Darren had similar thoughts and would have loved to inspect this so-called shed.

"Did you know the previous owner of this house?" Nesta asked.

"Of course," said Gemma. "I've been living on this street most of my life. She was Charlie's mother. Perhaps that's why I had a bit of a soft spot for her son."

"And what was *she* like?"

A sadness washed over Gemma's face. "Poor Alexandra. She was certainly a peculiar woman. Very different to her son."

Nesta was inclined to disagree but encouraged the woman to continue. "In what way?"

"She was very much a recluse for one thing. But a very pleasant woman if you met her. Talented, too. She did a lot of painting."

"I hear she was a descendant of the Delyn family," said Nesta.

Gemma shook her head. "She never liked to talk about that lot. Alexandra was something of a black sheep. She'd cut herself off a long time ago. Her brother still lives in Delyn House as far as I know. When their parents both died, Alexandra inherited enough to buy this place. She was already divorced by then. I believe she married a market trader from London. You can imagine how that would have gone down with a family like the Delyns."

"Charlie's father," said Nesta with a nod. "Was Charlie close with his mother?"

"I never saw him visit," said Gemma with a grave expression. "From what he told me, he seemed to hold a lot of resentment towards his family. Just like his mother did towards her I suppose. They were very similar in many ways."

"Did he resent his mother specifically?"

Gemma gave it some thought. "They hadn't spoken in years. I know Charlie used to say that he spent most of his childhood at boarding school. Like a lot of children from wealthy families like his, I suppose. He described being dropped off for the first time at a very early age. Nobody had explained to him where he was going. He'd spent his first day there doing puzzles in a book. Then, eventually, he went to find an adult and asked them when his parents were coming back to fetch him. They told him Christmas. He was about eight years old then."

Nesta felt her heart ache. She thought about her own children at that age and struggled to imagine not seeing them for such a great length of time. "Where did he go the rest of the time?"

"He used to spend the holidays with his father. His parents had separated when he was quite young."

"I did wonder," said Nesta. She recalled Charlie's memories of helping his father on the markets. It seemed that running a market stall was about more than making money for him. Nostalgia was a powerful thing. She would have been quite happy to spend a few hours helping out on a farm if it meant bringing back a slew of memories from her childhood.

The Beagle began sniffing at her leg, and she crouched down for a quick stroke.

"Reggie! Stop that!"

"It's alright," said Nesta. "I should be getting back to my own dog." She paused with a cringe and remembered the two cockapoos. "Or *dogs*, I should say."

The streetlights of Mold were burning bright, as the two visitors from Bala made their way back across town.

"We really should have checked out that shed," said Darren.

"And get arrested for trespassing?" asked Nesta. "I think we can be pretty confident about what's in there. Enough firepower to storm a military base by the sounds of it."

"Yeah, but the footage would have looked great." The teenager jiggled his phone. "You think Charlie was killed by a family member?"

Nesta looked up towards the clocktower of St Mary's Church. Its watchful eye had been following them the entire time. "Doesn't sound like there are many family members left. Charlie Coogan seems to have a lot of secrets in his life. And I don't believe we've heard them all just yet."

CHAPTER 17

Unlike her teenage lodger, Nesta was up bright and early on the Sunday morning. She had eaten breakfast, walked the dogs and even got some knitting in, all before Darren had emerged from his room.

"Are you coming to church?" Nesta asked, watching the bleary-eyed young man stumble down the stairs in the same clothes as the day before.

Darren stretched out his arms and checked his watch. This woman was far too energised for that time of the day, he thought. "You mean, to check the crime scene again?"

Nesta reached out her arms as if trying to reach the heavens. "I mean, to pay our respects to the Lord Almighty and worship him in his own house. There's a service on at eleven."

The word "service" had been enough to startle the teenager, who wanted to run a mile in the opposite direction. "You want to actually go to church?"

"Why not? It's a beautiful day for it. And you always feel better after going to church. Or at least I do. It's like a gym for the soul!"

The woman's overly cheerful mood was really starting to

grate on him now. Maybe he needed a coffee. "I think I'll stay outside and look for more clues. Get some more footage of the graveyard."

Nesta gave him a cynical stare. "Whatever floats your boat. Although, I wouldn't spend too much time filming gravestones. It can't be healthy." She watched him pour a bowl of cornflakes and immediately take a photograph with his phone. Perhaps there *were* stranger things, she thought.

∼

SITTING amongst the congregation of St Mary's Church, Nesta felt very much at home. She wouldn't have described herself as an overly religious person, but there was something about sharing a moment with a large group of people that brought her immense joy. She supposed that many people had a similar feeling whilst attending a music festival or, as her teenage friend would have preferred, a rowdy heavy metal concert.

Just like Charlie and his market stall, Nesta had been going to church since she was a little girl. Her parents had been regulars at Bala's very own Anglican church, and the whole experience of gazing around at the colourful stained glass windows transported her back every single time.

The Reverend Colin Johnson was a little more nervous than usual and had to keep wiping his sweaty brow after every few sentences of his sermon. By the time he had introduced the next hymn, his handkerchief was saturated, and he looked as though he were about to dunk his head into a fountain of holy water.

Nesta rose to her feet with her hymn book and looked out across a crowd of local regulars. She was surprised to have not seen anyone that she recognised, until a head full of fiery, red hair popped itself into view.

Wendy Stephens was only a couple of rows in front of her,

belting out the hymn with lungs that could power a foghorn. The proud baker could not hold a tune if her life depended on it, but that didn't seem to stop her singing her heart out.

Nesta waited until they had all gone up for communion, before she slipped into the empty seat beside her. "Fancy seeing you here."

Wendy turned to look at her as though people normally kept their distance. "Oh," she said. "Hello. What a nice surprise."

"Isn't it just?" Nesta lowered her voice to a whisper after a few of the people in front of them turned around with disapproving frowns. "I didn't realise you were a churchgoer."

Wendy raised up her chin with pride. "We all have to ensure our place through the gates of heaven. I'm willing to make sure I get a first class ticket."

Nesta had to prevent herself from laughing. She wasn't surprised in many ways. It was just like Wendy Stephens to completely miss the whole point of such a spiritual activity and start ticking boxes. If there was indeed a queue at the gates of heaven, she would have been happy to barge straight past everyone.

"So you come every Sunday?" Nesta asked.

"*Every* Sunday," Wendy snapped. "*And* special services."

"How impressive," Nesta muttered. "I'm sure you'll have plenty of brownie points with the man upstairs."

Wendy grinned. She couldn't agree more. "Talking of brownies..." The woman pointed to a large bag on the pew beside her. "I've baked up a special batch for our Reverend." She began gazing, lovingly, at the vicar, who was frantically wiping up a puddle of red wine he had just accidentally spilt. "He's so wonderful, isn't he?"

Nesta readjusted her glasses to make sure they were looking at the same person. "Who? The Reverend? Yes, I suppose he is a nice enough man."

"Can you believe he's not married?" Wendy asked, her eyes twinkling like the candles over on the altar. "Such a travesty." She tutted away, and the woman beside her began feeling very concerned for the unsuspecting vicar. There was a look in Wendy's eyes that reminded her of a cat that had just spotted its next meal. If anything could boost a person's chances of a happier afterlife, then surely it was marrying a vicar.

"It can't have been easy moving to a new town," said Nesta. "Colin seems to have settled in."

Wendy was struck by her use of the name "Colin". She was under the impression that only *she* had been on a first name basis with the man. "You know Colin?"

"Only very casually," said Nesta.

Wendy breathed a sigh of relief. "We've become quite close since he arrived. I've even had him round mine for afternoon tea."

Nesta wondered how much choice the poor man would have had in the matter and shuddered. "I've only spoken to him a couple of times," she continued. "He seemed to be quite close to Charlie as well."

Her observation caused the younger woman to loosen her straight posture into a disgruntled hunch. "Charlie Coogan?" Wendy scrunched up her mouth as though she were chewing on an over-baked sponge cake. "I wouldn't have said they were close. Charlie hardly even came to church. And when he did, he was usually skulking around in the back like a dark shadow."

Nesta could hear the venom in her voice and was curious to delve deeper. "Apparently the two had found some common ground. Charlie was struggling with his faith."

Wendy scoffed. "The last thing Colin needs is someone like that man by his side." She suddenly became aware of her own tone and lowered her voice. "I never like to speak ill of the dead, but that man was trouble." There was a pause, as she shifted her focus back to the vicar leading their service. "Not like Colin."

"I got the impression he was something of a war hero," said Nesta.

"Hardly," said Wendy with a groan. "You ever hear how he left the army?" A wicked smile crept across her face, when she realised that the other woman knew less than she did. "Dishonourable discharge."

"How do you know that?" asked Nesta, trying to hide her shock.

Wendy checked to make sure that nobody was listening. "I did a little bit of digging."

"On Charlie?"

"I was getting a little worried about how much time Colin was spending with this new friend of his. He cancelled on two of my afternoon teas."

Nesta rolled her eyes at her sudden change of tune regarding Colin and Charlie's relationship. It seemed that they *were* indeed close. "Go on," she said.

"Oh, it's not my place to say." Wendy began pretending to be invested in the service again before eventually adding: "It's really none of my business. But let's just say he didn't leave the army on good terms. And he was no hero."

They both stared at each other, as the opening bars of the next hymn rang in their ears.

Wendy smiled and turned to her hymn sheet. Nesta wanted to cover her ears, as she was forced to endure another bout of terrible singing.

After a long, disjointed sermon on one of his favourite bible passages, the Reverend Colin Johnson was relieved to bring his service to a close. It never seemed to get easier, and the nerves seemed to be ever-present for this young vicar with a reluctance for public speaking. Small talk was another personal issue, something that always proved unhelpful when bidding his congregation a friendly farewell.

"That was a lovely service," said Nesta, who had found the man quivering at the church entrance.

"Glad you could make it," said Colin, trying to avoid eye contact with a certain member of his local churchgoers. The woman with red hair had been anxiously waiting her turn for a quick word, and he had seen her coming from a mile off.

"Bravo!" Wendy cried, slipping herself in front of Nesta. "You have such a way with words."

"Oh," said the vicar, praying for her to leave, as she continued to encroach his personal space. "Thank you very much. I'm glad —"

"Do you like brownies?" asked Wendy. She lifted up her little care package and handed it to him.

"Oh, you really didn't have to —"

"I made three batches," said Wendy, breaking one of the brownies in half and placing it in her mouth. "Sometimes, you have to get the mixture just... right..."

Colin swallowed an enormous gulp. "You're very kind."

Wendy turned to look at Nesta with a smug grin. "I'll see you tomorrow evening for my next class." She turned to Colin with a toothy grin. "This is one of my baking students. There's plenty of room for improvement, but she tries hard. And that's the main thing." For a moment, she could have sworn she'd heard a pair of teeth grinding away beside her but thought nothing of it. "I'll see you in a mo for a quick chat."

The vicar felt his heart sink, and she blew him a kiss before walking away.

"I'm sure that it's people like Wendy who make the whole job worthwhile," said Nesta.

"Some people really like to devote their precious time to the church," said Colin, loosening his tight dog collar.

"How have you been coping?" asked Nesta. The man stared at her. "You know, with the loss of your friend."

"Oh, right. Yes. It's been... strange." He looked over in the direction of the area where Charlie Coogan was found only a few days before. "It's not easy having a constant reminder on your very own doorstep."

"I can only imagine. I was speaking to your groundskeeper yesterday. It was probably a shock for him, too. It's not every day you find a dead body in your workplace."

Colin shook his head and frowned. "Work is a strong word for that man. The agency charged us by the hour, and he'd hardly cut any grass at all. We won't be having him back again any time soon."

Nesta tried not to picture Jason Pott's miserable face, as he spoke about his recent unemployment. It did not sound good for him. "I'm very sorry to hear that." She suddenly became aware that there were other people behind her, waiting for their turn to speak with him. "I just had a quick question that I wanted to ask," she said.

The vicar lifted up his hand and signaled his openness. "Ask away. Answering questions is all part of the job."

"This is not about God," said Nesta. "I was wondering if Charlie ever talked about his time in the army."

"All the time," said Colin.

"Did he ever speak of any... difficulties?"

"Difficulties?" The man gave her an awkward smile. "Now, you know that everything a person tells me is in the strictest confidence."

"Yes," said Nesta. "But Charlie was a friend of yours, wasn't he?" She saw his discomfort and decided to change tact. "Listen, I'm not trying to pry, but did Charlie ever mention why he left the army?"

Colin gave his response some thought. "We talked about his

army days a lot. He once said that his time serving had been both a source of his faith and a reason for questioning it. Courage seemed to be a big topic."

"Courage?"

"Just the nature of it. What makes us brave. He often asked about God's views on the subject. We are all tested in this area at some point in our lives. I think Charlie was tested on more than one occasion. Some of the decisions he made in the past seemed to have haunted him. But it wasn't all doom and gloom. We also talked about love."

There it was, Nesta thought. That four letter word that caused so much trouble. "Was he ever married?"

Colin shook his head. "Not that I'm aware of. But there was someone from this town who he loved deeply. From what I gather, it was never meant to be."

"From Mold?"

The vicar ignored her question and appeared to be distracted by a figure over in the distance. Nesta cringed at the sight of Darren, who was busy rummaging amongst the tombstones with his phone.

"Isn't that a friend of yours?" Colin asked.

Nesta watched the teenager jumping around like a deranged rabbit, pointing his tiny lens at various graves. "Who, him?" She felt her cheeks go red. "No, that's just my nephew's son. Please forgive him. The poor lad's not long hit puberty."

CHAPTER 18

The graveyard at St Mary's church had returned to its usual quiet levels. People had deserted the main entrance after their regular Sunday fix of prayer and worship, all except two individuals who seemed to be more interested in the grave stones.

"Here's another one," said Darren.

Nesta walked over to find the name Elspeth Delyn carved into the hard stone. "She passed away three hundred years ago. I doubt she has much to do with what happened a few days ago."

The teenager was taken aback by her dismissive tone. "What's the matter with you?" he asked.

"I just feel we're missing a vital piece of information," said Nesta with a sigh. "I know that vicar was hiding something from me. There's more to Charlie's story. Something more recent. We're so focused on the past that we're missing clues from the present." She looked up towards the giant clock, as it let out its hourly chime. "That's it. We need to focus on *time*."

A confused Darren checked his watch. "You in a hurry now?"

"No," Nesta snapped. "I mean that we already have an exact time that the murder took place. The bell had just chimed before I heard the gunshot. That means we can rule a lot of people out, depending on their whereabouts at that exact time. I suppose it's pretty basic detective work, really, but it's easy to get sidetracked."

"What if the murder was committed by someone we haven't met?" Darren asked.

Nesta nodded. "A fair point. But we can only work with what we know. And everyone who Charlie knew. We have to start somewhere."

Darren looked up at the clock and stroked his chin. "You said the vicar was in the church. So that's one person ruled out."

Nesta shook her head. "He came running out of the church door *after* the gunshot, but that doesn't mean he was inside when it went off. He could have run back."

"Who else was around again?"

"There was the groundsman, who is in a similar boat as the vicar as far as his whereabouts is concerned. He appeared *after* the gunshot. Then there's Dorthy, who I saw down by the street when the gun went off."

Darren raised a cynical eyebrow. "That annoying old woman from the market? You're factoring *her* into all this?"

"We have to consider everyone," said Nesta. "No matter who they are." A thought popped into her head. "Actually, Dorothy could be useful. She might have seen someone we haven't considered yet heading into the church before I arrived. She's very observant."

"That's one word for it," Darren muttered.

"As far as the rest of this town goes, they all need a strong alibi for eleven o'clock. The further away from the church they were, the easier it is to rule them out."

"We could end up being in Mold all year! There's no way we can go through *everyone's* whereabouts."

Nesta turned to face him. "Where exactly were *you* when the gunshot went off?"

Darren could see the seriousness in her face, and his eyes widened. "Are you for real?" There was a long pause, until she burst out laughing.

"We have to consider *everyone*, Darren."

"Alright, where were *you* then?"

"Down by the road with Dorothy, remember? She's my alibi. I was with her when the gun went off."

The teenager folded up his arms in a sulk, until he remembered. "How many gunshots were there?"

Nesta could see the excitement in his eyes and reluctantly replied. "Just the one... why?"

Darren's beaming smile grew. "I found something."

They both made their way to the opposite side of the church which gave them a unique view of Mold's surrounding hills. Darren led the way towards one of the taller gravestones and pointed at his earlier find.

"Is that what I think it is?" asked Nesta.

"A bullet hole," Darren confirmed.

They both squinted at the damage and stuck their fingers into the tiny opening.

"We can't be certain," said Nesta.

A disappointed Darren frowned at her. "What else would have made that hole? A crazy woodpecker?"

Nesta turned around to face the line of enormous windows. They no longer possessed the vivid colours that she had seen from the inside. "Charlie was shot on the other side of the building. Unless he was killed with a magic bullet, there's no chance in a million years that it could have travelled into this gravestone."

Darren nodded. He couldn't argue with that logic. "Then there was a second shot."

"Impossible!" Nesta cried. "I would have heard it."

They both went quiet and did their best to come up with a more plausible solution. Unexpectedly for Darren, his little bullet mark had only served to complicate matters even more. It certainly hadn't got them any closer to solving Charlie's murder. "Maybe this gunshot was a completely separate day."

"If that's true," said Nesta, "then this place is more of a firing range than a church."

Darren stared into the hollow mark and was struck with an idea. "You know, there's one thing we haven't considered. What if Charlie had been shot by accident?" The woman opposite him waited for a further explanation. "What if someone was using this place as firing practice or something? Charlie might have been in the wrong place at the wrong time. Maybe the person who fired the gun never intended to kill anybody!"

Nesta let his words marinate for a while. He made a very good point, she thought. It was one of the best theories that they'd had so far, if only a little flawed. "Not bad," she said. "But why any maniac would ever choose the middle of Mold town centre to try out their firearm is beyond my understanding. Even if it was an accident, they're still a killer, and they clearly haven't turned themselves in."

"It all makes for a pretty boring conclusion to the video series, too," said Darren. "It's way more interesting if Charlie was killed by one of his enemies."

Nesta looked out across the street and saw a group of boisterous youths making their way down towards the traffic lights. Their rowdy cries could be heard even from the graveyard. "Who says it was just *one* enemy?" asked Nesta.

Darren tilted his head, and he reminded her of Hari when he was confused. Then, the young man saw that she was still staring at the noisy group over in the distance. He saw where her mind was going. "Like you were saying — who would be stupid enough to commit a crime in the middle of a public setting? Not just one person..."

Nesta turned back to face him and nodded. "What if it was a group?"

CHAPTER 19

Daniel Owen square hosted many events throughout the year, but *Rockamania* was unlike any other. Located in the centre of Mold, this celebration of good-old-fashioned rockabilly music attracted spectators from all over North Wales, many of them with pompadour haircuts and shirts that rarely saw the light of day.

As well as a purposely built stage that dominated a quarter of the square, there were food stalls, a bar and even some nostalgic memorabilia on sale.

"I thought you said this was a rock concert," said Darren, standing at the back of the crowd. He stared at the warm-up act with a cynical frown. As far as he was concerned, a banjo had no place in the type of rock music that *he* listened to. If there were no power chords or electric guitar solos, then it might as well have been psychedelic trance.

"They're playing bluegrass," said Nesta, tapping her foot. She saw the blank stare and sighed. "This is a celebration of the entire genre! We're talking about the birth of rock as we know it. Country, rhythm and blues, soul… it didn't all start with heavy metal, you know?"

"It definitely finished with it," Darren muttered, folding up his arms.

Nesta refused to let her grumpy companion ruin her fun and began swinging her hips in time with the music. Her impromptu dance caused a surge of embarrassment with the disapproving teenager, and he decided to excuse himself as quickly as possible. "I'm going to find something to eat," he said and headed off towards the back of the square.

Darren weaved through the crowds of locals and recognised many of the faces from his time on the stall. It was incredible how familiar people became after spending enough time in the same place. He saw the man with his two giant dogs (who always seemed to be more in control than he was). There was the loud, angry mother with her five children — and the even angrier husband that she loved to bicker with. Even Dorothy was out and about, sitting on her bench, watching the world go by.

All that time on the stall had turned him into an avid people-watcher, just like Nesta. A slightly disturbing thought was the fact that, somewhere, lurking amongst that crowd of people was a killer, and it was enough to put him off the enormous burgers he had been eyeing off since they arrived.

Out of all the familiar attendees of the annual Mold *Rockamania* festival, the one person he had not expected to see was a teenager from his own hometown.

"Darren!" Lowri Meredydd cried.

"Lowri?" Darren asked, turning around to see his fellow English classmate waving at him. He was used to seeing her in school uniform, but today she was in jeans and a t-shirt with her hair let loose. "What are you doing here?" He couldn't help but notice the stand-offish male teenager by her side and hoped he was just a relative. Despite his past rejection, he still hadn't given up on the most beautiful girl in his year.

"I'm staying here with my cousin," said Lowri.

Darren breathed a sigh of relief and waved at the teenager beside her. "Nice to meet you."

The young man sniggered and Lowri gave him a playful nudge. "Not him," Lowri said with a giggle. "He's not my cousin."

"Oh," said Darren. His face went bright red, and his relief turned back to dread.

"This is Jay." Her flirtatious gaze at the boy in designer clothes told everything Darren needed to know, and his heart sank. The name "Jay" reminded him of the cockapoos: Taylor, Kim and Jay — they would have made a perfect trio, he thought.

"So, you like rockabilly?" Jay asked with a smirk.

Darren became reminded of where he was and scoffed. "What, this music? Nah. I'm just in town for a bit. Thought I'd swing by and see what all the fuss was about."

"I think it's fun," said Lowri. "We don't have anything like this back home."

"We've got Sioe Bala," said Darren (more defensively than he had intended). "And the fair. That's twice a year."

The couple in front of him giggled, much to his annoyance.

"Don't forget the Eisteddfod," said Lowri.

Darren couldn't work out whether she was being serious and decided not to respond.

"So where's your girlfriend at, Bala-boy?" asked Jay.

"Jay!" Lowri cried and gave him a nudge.

Jay raised up his arms. "What? He might have one. Lone Ranger like him, rolling into town."

"Well, actually, I —" Just as Darren stumbled out his words in a desperate attempt to redeem himself, he was patted on the back by a lively young woman, who proceeded to put an arm around him. "Alright, sunshine?" Claire combed back her purple hair and rolled up her sleeve. "Ready for my big film shoot?"

Darren saw the dumbfounded looks on Lowri and Jay and could not have been more grateful. He puffed out his chest and decided to milk the moment for as long as he could. "Yeah, sure. We can shoot some takes later, if you like?"

"Perfect," said Claire. "I'm off to get my new tattoo finished. I'll give you a bell when I'm done."

"Yeah, catch you later." Darren gave her a quick high-five before she headed off and turned back to the silent couple.

"What's that about a film shoot?" asked Lowri.

Darren batted her question away as if it were nothing. "Don't really have time to go into it now," he said. "As you can see, I've got a lot on today. Need to grab some chow. You kids have fun."

He swaggered off into the crowd and left the pair confused.

Meanwhile, Nesta was still bobbing away to the lively music. The warm-up act had reached its final song, and she raised her hands up in the air for an applause.

Next up were The Gaggles, and she watched a confident Mark Hutson stroll across the stage with his trusty guitar. Like many of his audience members, the record stall owner had slicked up the front of his hair and was dressed in a shirt louder than his music.

"Good afternoon, Mold!" he cried out. The wave of cheers caused him to smile and wink, whilst the rest of his band picked up their instruments and prepared to rock the entire square.

Nesta could see a woman leaping up and down in the front row and realised it was Wendy. Of course Wendy was in the front row, she thought, having had enough of her baking teacher for one day. Her gaze hovered over the rest of the crowd, and she cast her mind back to that scene in The Conversation. What a surveillance person she would have made, and if only she could have listened in to each little verbal exchange like a fly on the wall who had decided to go further afield. Curiosity killed the cat, but Nesta was more of a dog person.

Moving through the crowd was Jake, the baker's son. The teenager had made quite the effort and was dressed in his best (and only) shirt. He seemed to be searching for someone, and she followed his movements across the square.

Eventually, he spotted someone standing beside the burger van. The young woman in a light, summer dress greeted him with an excited smile. They both hugged and began chatting and laughing with each other.

Nesta witnessed the whole exchange with a smile. Young love, she thought. How wonderful it was.

The conversation between the teenagers continued, until they were approached by a familiar young man in a loose tracksuit. Nesta recognised him as Archie, the youth whose friends had tried to steal from her stall. The conversation between him and Jake appeared to get heated very quickly, and, eventually, the baker's son was shoved backwards, causing him to trip over a small dustbin.

Nesta gasped, and watched the embarrassed young man dust himself off and climb to his feet. When it seemed like he was going to strike back, Jake hesitated and headed back through the crowd in the opposite direction. The young woman called after him, whilst Archie laughed and shook his head.

Jake continued his emotional march that took him out of the square and into the narrow side street. The surrounding shops were all closed, and he heard an unexpected voice calling out to him. "Wait!" He turned around to see Nesta running towards him. She took a moment to catch her breath. "It's Jake, isn't it?"

The confused young man was still rattled from his encounter in the square and struggled to find the words to respond. "Uh, yeah. Who's asking?"

"I was talking to your father yesterday, remember? I bought a Manchester tart from you."

Jake nodded and the penny dropped. "Oh, aye. Sure. This is not a good time."

"I saw what just happened."

The teenager froze, just as he was about to make himself scarce. He stared back into her knowing eyes.

"That young man you were talking to in the square," Nesta continued, "he's trouble, that one."

"Yeah, tell me about it." Jake loosened his crumpled-up collar. "I wouldn't say he was a mate."

"But that young woman was." Nesta studied his reaction, as he could tell what she was implying. "You seemed to be getting on very well."

Jake was now even more uncomfortable. "Emma and I are just —"

"Friends? Archie didn't seem to think so."

The young man looked around, but there was nobody watching. Everyone was far too interested in the man swinging his hips on the stage than hanging around in an empty sidestreet. "How do you know his name?"

"I asked around," said Nesta. "That little weasel tried to steal from my stall. Him and his little minion friends."

Jake nodded. "Sounds about right. But I wouldn't say that he's the ringleader. Not by a long shot. He used to be scared of his own shadow until he started hanging around with that lot. And they used to treat him like dirt until recently."

"You've known him a long time?"

"Since we were in nursery," said Jake. "Then primary school. But we went to separate secondary schools. Archie was always picked on, mainly because of his size. He was crap at sports. And whenever he got into fights, he'd either lose or walk away crying."

Nesta listened with great surprise. "He seemed very confident with you just now."

Jake frowned. "That's just because — I can't say." He clenched his fists as though he wanted to take out his frustrations on a brick wall. "He seems to think Emma's his girlfriend.

But it's obvious she doesn't even fancy him. Why would anyone fancy a weedy little shrimp like him? You could snap him like a twig."

"Then why were you so scared of him?"

Nesta's question cut straight through him, just as she had intended. There had been a look on his face when confronted with Archie that screamed fear, even from all the way across the square. "I'm not scared of *him*. It's what everyone says he's got."

"He threatened you, didn't he?" Nesta asked again. "With what?"

Jake struggled to say the words. "He's got — he's got a gun."

CHAPTER 20

"How did he know the guy's got a gun?"

Darren was just about to bite into his piping-hot burger, when he waited for the response.

"Apparently," said Nesta, "this Archie lad has told everyone. He's not the smartest tool in the box." She lifted up her own burger and went in for a large mouthful.

They both sat on a circular bench that surrounded a small tree at the edge of Daniel Owen square. There were three of these trees in total, and each one provided the ideal amount of shade from the summer sun. The burgers had been a long time coming, and both of them savoured every morsel whilst listening to the latest act.

Mark and his Gaggles were still jamming away on stage, and the residents of Mold continued to hover around the square like curious insects.

"Do you think it's true?" asked Darren.

Nesta licked some stray ketchup off her thumb. "Jake said he's seen a photo of it. He showed me on his phone. It looked like an old pistol."

"How old?"

"Older than me, probably, if that helps." Nesta chuckled.

"Not really," said Darren. "That means it could be ancient." He felt a screwed up burger wrapper *whack* him in the head. "Only joking, obviously..."

"I'm no gun expert," Nesta continued. "But I've seen that type of gun before. Couldn't tell you where."

"Might be a fake," Darren muttered.

"I don't blame Jake for not wanting to take the chance. He seemed nervous around Archie." She swallowed the last of her burger and shook her head. "It sounds strange, though. What youth goes around with a gun in this country? Of all the weapons... it's a bit of a coincidence." She turned to see Darren flicking through his mobile phone and sighed. "I should have known you weren't listening."

"I'm looking up old handguns," the teenager snapped. "See if I can jog your memory."

"My memory's just fine, thank you very much." Nesta budged up so that she could see his screen, and she watched him scan through a series of images. "There!" she cried. Darren's finger froze. "That's the one he showed me. It's identical."

Darren squinted at his screen and began reading the description: "A PPK — semi-automatic pistol. Made in Germany in nineteen-thirty-one. Not as old as you, then." He felt a sharp pinch and yelped out with a smirk. "Used by the army during World War II. It was the weapon used by Adolf Hitler to commit suicide. It became famous thanks to the fictional character of James Bond, who has used it in many of his films, where he attaches a silencer to the barrel when a subtle job is required..."

"Yes!" Nesta cried. "That's where I've seen it before. My Morgan used to love the Bond films. We'd always watch them if they were on the telly."

"The *Mission Impossible* films are better," Darren muttered.

"That little Tom Cruise?" Nesta scoffed. "No wonder his

missions are impossible. He's far too pretty to be a spy."

They gathered around the phone screen, staring at the historical pistol.

Nesta slipped on her glasses and stared at the weapon's elegant design. "What on earth is a teenager in Mold doing with one of those?"

"It could be a replica," said Darren. "Might have got it from a toy shop."

The woman beside him wasn't so certain. If it were indeed a fake, she thought, then why not get something more formidable or modern? Like a revolver? Or at least a magnum? If it was intended to intimidate people, then why get something so small?

"I think we need to confirm that Archie's whereabouts at the time that Charlie was shot," she said.

Darren turned to her in surprise. "You reckon that weedy lad with baggy trousers killed Charlie?"

"It's worth ruling him out," said Nesta. "So far, he's the only person we can confirm that has access to a firearm."

"What about that fruit and veg lady?"

"True." Nesta nodded. There were a lot more guns in Flintshire than a person would think. Mold really *was* beginning to feel like the Wild West, and she never thought she would be saying that.

"I thought you said the gunshot sounded like a rifle?" asked Darren.

Nesta shrugged. "A *bang*'s a *bang*, I suppose. I've been mistaken before. Plus, my hearing's not what it used to be."

Darren agreed with both of those last two facts but didn't dare mention it.

"If only we had a way of knowing exactly who was near the church at eleven o'clock on the day Charlie died," Nesta said.

"Like CCTV footage or something?" Darren asked. "I bet you

the police have some."

"Surveillance footage would be perfect," said Nesta with a sigh. "Unfortunately, this is not a perfect world." She gazed around the crowd of people filling up the entire square. Her eyes scanned the various, happy faces, all enjoying their afternoon of live music, until they fell on a figure sitting on the bench only a couple of trees along. Nesta smiled. "On the other hand... who needs a clunky surveillance camera when you have a living, breathing one?"

Darren watched her head over to the elderly woman three benches down and realised that she had been referring to Dorothy.

"Mind if I join you?" Nesta asked.

Dorothy looked up with a smile. "Be my guest. It's a free country."

Nesta sat down beside her, and they both looked out across the busy square.

"I like this town," she said, eventually. "There's all kinds of different people here. Plenty to do and see."

"Oh, yes." Dorothy could not have agreed more. "I've lived in Mold all my life. I know the place backwards. Every inch of it."

"You must have seen all sorts over the years," said Nesta. "People rarely just stop to sit in one place nowadays. Everyone's always in a rush. They always need to be distracted. Nobody just sits in silence and listens to their own thoughts." She watched a young man go past with a pair of enormous headphones and another who was walking whilst messaging on his phone.

Both women realised that they were watching the same thing and turned to each other with a laugh.

"They're missing what's right in front of them," said Dorothy. "There's already so much to take in." She nodded to a passing local, who waved at her.

"Exactly," said Nesta. "What's the point of our eyes and ears

The Mystery At Mold Market 159

if we're not using them in the real world?"

Dorothy chuckled. She was beginning to like this woman. "We sound like a right pair of old codgers now."

Nesta pointed towards the rock and roll group, shaking their hips onstage. "Who, us? We're at a rock concert, for goodness sake. These youngsters have no idea what's hit them."

"My husband used to like his rock music," said Dorothy.

"So did mine," said Nesta. "Elvis, specifically."

Dorothy gave her a nod of approval. "Ah, you can't beat the king himself."

"It's a shame my Morgan isn't still around to appreciate this concert. He would have loved this."

"Aye," said Dorothy. "I know what you mean." She glanced at the other woman's sad face and could sense (as only a fellow widow could) exactly what she was feeling.

Nesta had noticed that Dorothy was in a more solemn mood that afternoon. She had previously come across as a little manic and eccentric, but it seemed that there was a quieter side to this Mold local.

"Oi!!" Dorothy cried out at a passing young man with a hot dog in his hand. "You!! How much did you pay for that hot dog?"

The man paused and looked over with a confused frown. "Uh, about a fiver I think."

Dorothy wailed like an excited crow. "Argh! You were ripped off! They robbed you blind!"

Nesta took her previous thoughts back about the woman beside her and concluded that she really was a little eccentric, after all.

"I wanted to ask you," she said. "Do you remember when we bumped into each other outside the church?"

Dorothy gave her a blank stare. "Church? What church?"

"The big one... over on the high street."

"Oh! Yes. *That* church. It's very nice, have you seen it?"

Nesta tried to remain calm. "Yes. I was walking past it with my dogs the other day, remember? You were sitting by the main road outside it." Despite her previous conversation about surveillance cameras, at least a piece of CCTV hardware did not require reasoning with, she thought.

"The dogs!" Dorothy cried. "They were giving you a right hard time. Those beautiful cockapoos. And the Jack Russell."

"Yes!" Nesta cried out, struggling to contain her excitement at a breakthrough. "That was it. Now, do you remember seeing anyone else head into the church? Before I arrived? Before the loud *bang*?"

"*Bang*?" Dorothy chuckled. "I think you might be going a bit funny, dear."

Nesta sighed and noticed the woman's hearing aids. She had forgotten about those. "What I mean is — did you see anyone else around? Anyone else at all, besides me?"

Dorothy tried to think and gave her question some serious thought. "Now, let me see..." The anticipation was killing the woman beside her, who was about to hang on every next word that came out of her mouth. "There was Sharon from the hairdressers — she walked past."

"Did she go through the church gates?"

"Oh, no. She was walking on the other side of the road."

Nesta took a deep breath. "Okay, was there anyone else? Anyone else that actually went towards the church?"

"The church? Why would they go in there?"

"But was there someone who *did*?"

Dorothy shook her head. "No, I don't recall anyone going to church. Except those little doggies taking you for a walk!" She chuckled. "Wait! There was that man in the flashy coat."

Her words ignited a burning fire of hope in Nesta's eyes. "Flashy coat? You mean the groundskeeper? Jason Potts?"

"Ah, yes. Little Jason Potts." Dorothy's heart melted. "I used to teach him in school. Hopeless, he was. But I always liked his mother."

Nesta's mouth stumbled from the onslaught of questions that wanted to escape it. "Wait — what? You were a teacher?"

Dorothy nodded. "Oh, aye. I was a history teacher." The woman tapped the side of her head. "I've got a very good long term memory, you know. Good for dates."

The fellow retired teacher had to ignore the last few comments and keep their conversation on track. "Okay, so you saw little Jason Potts?" Nesta didn't bother to point out that the man certainly was not so little anymore. "He walked past you from the street?"

"Just after you did," said Dorothy. "He seemed in a terrible rush."

"*After* I went past?" Nesta had to shake her head to keep her thoughts together. "You're certain it was *after*?"

"Oh, yes." Dorothy smiled and tapped her temple again. "I've got a very good memory, remember?"

Nesta went quiet for a moment. It didn't make any sense, she thought. Jason Potts was supposed to be around the back of the church cutting the grass. If what Dorothy had just said was true, then Jason had lied to her — and lies were usually a cause for concern.

She climbed to her feet and bid the woman a quick farewell.

"Going so soon?" Dorothy asked, having been grateful for the company.

"I need to get back to my friend over there," said Nesta. Darren had finished his burger and looked as though he were about to drift off from the overdose of rockabilly music. "He doesn't get out very much."

"Wait!" Dorothy cried, as she tried to walk away. Nesta turned around to see her excited face. "I haven't told you about the teenagers!"

CHAPTER 21

Before the time had come for Darren to catch the last bus back to Bala, Nesta had managed to fill the teenager in on her conversation with Dorothy. The sighting of the "teenagers" had further cemented their growing theory involving a young man and his historical pistol. Despite her often fractured short-term memory, Dorothy's recall for names was impeccable. She knew most people in the town of Mold and could recite the forenames of their children and grandchildren with relative ease.

As a former teacher herself, Nesta understood this skill very well. It was easy to navigate the younger generation when you had taught all of their parents (and, in some cases, dare she say it — grandparents). You didn't need a website like *Lineage* when you already had a mind full of family trees growing away. These were the sort of details that stuck, and no amount of short-term memory lapses could lose those. Local knowledge really was invaluable, Nesta had come to realise, especially when trying to navigate a murder case. She wasn't in Bala anymore, and any details that an out-of-towner like her could use were most welcome.

"She saw Archie?" Daren asked, whilst they waited beside the empty bus stop.

"And two others called Harry and Macsen," said Nesta. "She knew their parents and said that they're all the spitting image."

Darren shook his head. "I don't know how we can trust anything that woman says. She's barking mad. It's not exactly concrete evidence."

"She might be a little scatty, but there's a strong mind in there. I can tell. I know it's hard for someone like you to believe, but aging happens to all of us. And, unfortunately, it takes its toll on both the body and mind." Nesta stretched out her arm to make a loud *crack*. "I feel incredibly lucky so far. The body might be going downhill, but I'm still okay up in the old temporal lobe, thankfully." She tapped her head.

"I wouldn't go that far," said Darren with a cheeky grin. He received a well-deserved thump on the arm.

"The brain is a remarkable thing," Nesta continued. "And it's also very resilient. Dorothy's is no different. I believe what she saw."

Darren sighed. "Okay, so what exactly *did* she see?"

"She watched the three teenagers entering through the church entrance. Now, I hate to make assumptions, but Archie and his pals don't seem like regular churchgoers. So, it's highly suspicious. Plus, Charlie was probably not popular with some of the more antisocial youths of this town. Give the young ones a handgun, and it's a recipe for disaster."

They both turned to see the bus approaching.

"So what now?" asked Darren. "We confront Archie?"

"Not yet," said Nesta. "We need to be certain."

The T8 towards Corwen car park pulled up beside them, and the teenager prepared to board. "Right," he said. "I'll see you for the Wednesday market. Try not to get into too much trouble before then."

Nesta smiled. "Oh, I can't promise you that."

～

On Monday morning, Nesta had decided it was about time that she visited Mold's museum, which, rather conveniently, also happened to be situated above the library. After all, Charlie Coogan himself had recommended that she take a look, and Nesta was not disappointed.

Welsh history had always fascinated her, particularly the parts she was unfamiliar with. Stepping back in time to the days of novelist Daniel Owen, who had his very own reconstructed study, was an absolute pleasure. She read all about the famous gold cape, a ceremonial piece dating back to the Bronze Age, as well as a quick detour to Norman times, where the foundations of Bailey Hill had been placed down in an attempt to thwart off various armies and invaders.

It had all been a lot to take in before lunchtime, and Nesta decided to relax her mind with a quick visit to the library. She wasn't the only person to find solace in a spot of fictional reading and found many of the town's residents sitting around in blissful silence. To her great surprise, she realised that the selection of crime books at Mold library was far more extensive than her usual selection and, for a moment, debated the sheer madness of taking out a second library card.

"Hello," said the cheerful librarian, as she passed by Nesta's table with a pile of books in her hand.

"Oh," said Nesta, as she looked up at the familiar face. "It's *you!*"

Millie Hogan, who could normally be found selling dream catchers and tarot cards on her market stall, gave her that wholesome smile that seemed to radiate positivity like one of her scented candles. "Enjoying a spot of light reading?"

Nesta saw that she was referring to the book in her hand entitled: *Weapons of World War II*. She had been meaning to pick up a few adventures that followed her favourite Italian detective, Inspector Montalbano, but the cover of the more practical book about British and German firearms had been too hard to resist.

"Just a little hobby of mine," said a blushing Nesta, closing up the book. "I didn't know that you worked here."

"Ah," said Millie. "Unfortunately, two days a week on the market doesn't quite pay the bills. I have a few jobs in this town." She looked around at the room full of quiet readers. "It's a pretty good gig. Although, the toddler and baby classes can get a bit stressful when there's a lot of tears."

"I can only imagine," said Nesta. She was rather jealous, having often thought that she would make a good librarian. The retired teacher had experienced an entire career of hushing people, and the unprecedented daily access to books sounded like a dream. "I've just been upstairs to the museum."

Millie nodded with approval. "It's fairly new. Fascinating history, isn't it? I often go up on my lunch break."

Nesta would have thought that a library was a more suitable place to spend one's work break (although, if a person's job was organising books, then perhaps not). "Yes, I had no idea Mold was so historical. There is one part of its history, though, that I wanted to get a little more familiar with but have struggled. And I can't seem to find any books on the subject."

Millie placed down her pile of books. "Oh? Maybe I can help. I've lived here all of my life."

"The Delyn family," said Nesta. "I take it you've heard of them?"

The librarian's eyes lit up. "Of course! They've been around for centuries. There's a large country house just outside of town. It's not open to the public, sadly. But one of the Delyns still resides there." She let out a mischievous smile. "There's a rumour in my family that we might be related somehow. My uncle worked it out once, but I couldn't tell you how."

"Is that right?" asked Nesta.

"My sister works there, actually. My uncle was so obsessed with he family history that he struck up a relationship with the lord. Uncle Paul's a budding writer, you see. He wanted to write a book on the Delyns, and the lord was happy to oblige. That's how my sister landed the job there. She's the housekeeper now."

Nesta couldn't believe her luck. It was as though this woman was some mystical oracle that she had been destined to bump into. Perhaps Millie sold dream catchers and tarot cards for a reason. "What a small town this is."

"You have no idea," said Millie with a grin.

"That nugget you sold me," Nesta said. "It seems to be bringing me a tremendous amount of luck. I might need to buy another one."

Millie was flattered and failed to hide it. "Really? Oh, I'm so pleased. I'll have to give you a link to my online shop so you can leave a review!"

The words "online" and "link" were enough to make Nesta sick, but she refused to show it. "Of course. Actually, I was just wondering about your sister — do you think you could put me in contact with her?"

CHAPTER 22

The last time Nesta had visited a large country house, she had unearthed a whole box of secrets that solved the most cold-blooded murder case that she had yet to encounter. This time, the circumstances of her visit were quite different. For one thing, she was not arriving unannounced, having arranged to meet with Millie Hogan's sister, Daphne, who was more than happy to give her guest a little tour of the grounds.

Nesta was not expecting quite the revelation of her visit to Picton Hall but hoped that she could at least get a chance to speak with the lord himself this time.

Charlie Coogan had taken quite an interest in the Delyn branch of his family tree, and if there was anything she knew about the members of the landed gentry, it was that they could be a ruthless bunch when it came to their inheritance (at least according to Agatha Christie).

The gates of Delyn House were wide open when her little Citroën approached, and she drove through them with a certain degree of smugness. It wasn't every day that she could visit a property this grand without the help of her *National Trust* card.

The narrow road curved its way past a series of perfectly-cut lawns, all crying out for a game of croquet. Looking at the state of the pristine gardens, she was glad to have left her three dogs at home for this trip, as the cockapoos would have had a field day and were not to be trusted.

Delyn House's sweeping gravel drive was lined with trees that led all the way to a turning circle outside the main entrance. The arched windows of this two-storey building were surrounded by elegant brickwork, and the facade was dominated by a green door made of solid timber.

Nesta pulled up into the driveway and gazed out at the miles of open countryside stretching out into the distance beyond the surrounding ha-ha wall. She would have been quite happy living in such a house if it weren't for the sheer amount of hoovering and mowing required.

Stepping out into the warm air, Nesta spotted a groundskeeper making his way across the lawn with a full wheelbarrow.

"Hey!" she cried out and went scurrying towards him. "You!!"

Jason Potts was just starting to enjoy the tranquility of his new job, when he looked up to see a furious figure heading towards him. He wanted desperately to run away when he recognised the face, but there was nowhere to hide in the grounds of Delyn House.

"You lied to me," Nesta hissed, as she approached the surprised man and tried to catch her breath.

"What are you doing here?" asked Jason. "You been following me?"

Nesta frowned and placed both hands against the side of her hips. "Excuse me? I'll have you know that I have an engagement at this here house. I think the more appropriate question is what are *you* doing here?"

"I work here now," said Jason. He received a suspicious stare.

"Don't you think it's a little bit of a coincidence?" asked Nesta.

"Well, it wasn't until you turned up. I was here first. Plus, I don't appreciate being called a liar."

Nesta's frown deepened. "Really? Then why did you tell me that you were at the back of the church when Charlie Coogan was shot? I have a key witness that saw you entering from the street shortly after the gunshot."

"Ah," said Jason, looking very guilty. "Aye, I might have not been a hundred percent honest on that one."

Nesta rolled her eyes. "Okay. Then where exactly were you?"

Jason took a quick look over her shoulder to make sure that his new employer was still inside the house. "Listen, I wasn't gone for long, but there was this bet I needed to put on..." Judging by the look on the woman's face, he barely needed to continue. "I know what you're thinking. You think I've got a problem."

Nesta folded up her arms. "Trust me. You don't want to know what I'm thinking."

The groundskeeper lowered his head in shame. "Yeah, well. You'd understand if you knew how skint I've been. This bet was a done deal. It was worth a month's wages." He let out a smug grin. "Plus, it worked, too. It was a three-nil win." Jason saw that the woman didn't seem to share in his excitement. "Anyway, I parked the lawn mower and snuck off to the bookies. I even left her running. I wasn't planning on being gone long."

Nesta listened with a slight feeling of disappointment. His excuse sounded highly likely, especially for a gambler like Jason. "Don't worry," she said. "I won't tell your employer."

Jason breathed a sigh of relief. "Oh, ta. That's much appreciated."

She leant forward into his personal space. "But I do have a

few questions." The man's heart sank. "Did you see anyone else around the church that day?"

The man scratched his head. "I saw the vicar, obviously. He was a bit of a micro-manager, to be honest. It's only cutting grass, like, but he had a particular way he wanted it doing."

"Anyone else?"

"Uh, there were a couple of tourists at one point," said Jason. "American, I think."

The mention of America intrigued Nesta. They were, after all, a nation that carried more than their fair share of firearms. She had never met one, but it was hard not to draw a stereotype. She imagined cowboy hats and giant moustaches, before realising how ludicrous her own mind was. Charlie's death was never going to be the result of a dramatic showdown at sundown (even though it would have been an exciting conclusion and one that Darren would have absolutely relished). "What did these Americans look like — I mean, how long were they hanging around for?"

"Not long," said Jason. "They took a few photos and asked me where the castle was. I had to explain that Bailey Hill wasn't really an actual castle, mind, but that didn't seem to stop them."

A disappointed Nesta nodded. She had squeezed enough blood out of this unhelpful stone, and now it was time to move on.

"Oh," said Jason, as she began walking away. "I did come across this one thing you might find interesting. Well, I did anyway." Nesta turned around and waited for him to elaborate. "I found something in the grass. Probably would have mowed the thing over if the police hadn't been called. I showed it to them, obviously, in case it was related to the shooting. I took a picture." He pulled out his phone and began rooting through his recent images.

Nesta peered down and saw a metallic cylinder lying in the grass.

Jason tapped his large finger against the photograph. "You know what that is?" he asked.

The woman gazing at his phone screen nodded. "Yes, I think I do."

"Oh, heck." The groundskeeper stuffed his phone back into his coat. "You're going to get me sacked if you're not careful."

Nesta saw that he had noticed a woman emerging from the house.

"She's a right taskmaster," said Jason. "That's the housekeeper."

Daphne Hogan waited for Nesta to make the long walk back across the lawn. She was the spitting image of her sister, Millie, only with a more formal attire.

"Nesta?" she asked.

∽

"I don't normally do these sort of things," said Daphne after they had walked around the final section of the gardens. "But my sister loves telling people where I work."

"Yes," said Nesta, who had enjoyed every minute of her private tour so far. The gardens had been beyond her initial expectations for such an unknown country house with its neatly-clipped box hedges and symmetrical parterres. There had been flowers that she recognised, such as roses and delphiniums, as well as plenty that she had never even seen before. They had even passed through a high-brick walled garden with its own Victorian-style glass house and circular fish pond. "Your sister is very proud."

Daphne scoffed. "I wouldn't go that far. She's not exactly

traditional, my sister. My uncle describes her as being 'off with the fairies'."

"Is this the same uncle who's been researching your family history?" asked Nesta.

"That's the one," said Daphne with a groan. "He was very excited when I started working here. Gave him an excuse to visit every five minutes. I told him he should get a job here himself. But he's only ever worked in offices all his life. Couldn't do anything manual if he tried."

Nesta followed the woman through into another section of the walled garden. "Millie reminds me a lot of my own sister," she said, thinking about Mari. "She was often described as the hippy of the family."

"Hippy is probably a good word," said Daphne. "Anyone who tries to make a living selling voodoo perfumes is definitely on another planet to the rest of us. I don't know how she does it. As you can see, we're quite different people. Even though we might look similar."

"Mari and I are hardly two peas in a pod either," said Nesta. "Although, sometimes I wish I could be a little more like her. Ying, yang and all of that. I'm trying to have a little more adventure in my life these days. Life can get very serious if you let it."

A cynical Daphne wasn't quite so sure. "Now *you're* beginning to sound like the hippy."

Nesta looked up towards the house. "Do you think we can have a little look inside?" Daphne checked her watch. "I don't want to disturb the lord if he's in or anything."

"Lord Delyn?" asked Daphne. "I'm not worried about disturbing *him*. He loves a visitor. That's the problem. Once he starts talking, you'll never escape. We had a plumber in the other day, and the poor guy was stuck for hours."

"So he's quite lonely?"

"It's hardly surprising, living in a place like this. He never leaves the grounds anymore. Unfortunately, it means that his staff have to put up with his dithering. I don't get paid enough sometimes. I'm not a carer."

Nesta's face lit up. "Perhaps I can keep him busy for you then. Might give you an hour's peace. I'd love to meet him."

Daphne looked at her as though she was stark-raving mad. "Don't say I didn't warn you. Oh, and whatever you do, don't mention anything to do with the military. Or you'll start him off again."

Five minutes later, and they were both making their way inside the house. Nesta crossed through into the oak-panelled entrance hall and was struck with that familiar smell of polished wood and old stone. These ancient homes were like a time capsule, and she immediately began admiring a series of old tapestries.

What struck her the most was not the centuries of history, but the sound of music echoing around the walls.

Daphne led the way past a line of mullioned windows overlooking the gardens. The classical music became louder with each step, and Nesta began to wonder whether the estate had its very own resident orchestra.

Once they had reached the drawing room, the source of the noise was soon revealed, and there was not one musician in sight.

Daphne stopped at the open doorway and shook her head in disapproval. "He always does this on a Tuesday," she muttered. "It's no wonder he's going deaf."

Standing with his back to them was an elderly gentleman dressed in a ceremonial suit. He swung his arms around like a classical conductor, as the record player in front blasted out a dramatic song.

Nesta entered the room and admired the elegant furniture before waiting for the music to die down.

""Ride Of The Valkyries"," she said. "Nothing like a bit of Wagner to get the blood pumping."

Her words startled the old lord, who swung himself around so quickly that he nearly toppled over.

"Good heavens!" Lord Delyn cried. "You scared the life out of me." He stroked his white moustache and squinted at the woman standing in the middle of his living room. "Daphne! Why didn't you tell me we had guests!"

The housekeeper rolled her eyes and walked away.

Lord Delyn strutted his way across the room and shook Nesta's hand. "Anyone with musical taste like yours is more than welcome in this house." He gave her hand a kiss, and she was happy to be charmed.

"I wouldn't say I'm an expert," said Nesta. "The last time I heard Wagner, I was on hold with my gas provider."

The man chuckled, and he scurried over to turn off his record player. "I bet a spring chicken like yourself hasn't seen one of these in a while." He removed the record and twirled it in his hand.

Nesta smiled. Flattery would get him everywhere. "You'd be surprised. Vinyl's really coming back into fashion now. There's a man down at Mold market who can sort you out. In fact, I believe your nephew collected a few."

Lord Delyn's eyes widened. "Charlie-boy?"

Nesta studied his reaction. It appeared to be one of great sadness, and she decided to give him a moment. "I had the great pleasure of meeting him before he died," she said, eventually. "I'm sorry for your loss."

The man's jovial mood had vanished, and he began pacing back and forth. "Dear, dear. My poor Charlie. I'm so pleased that my sister didn't have to be here to witness this terrible tragedy. God rest her soul."

"Am I right in thinking that your sister had a tendency to keep to herself?"

Lord Delyn gave a heavy nod. "We hadn't spoken for a very long time. She had always been distant. Hated family gatherings of any kind." He looked up at the ceiling. "I think she resented the fact that this house was left to me when our father died. I don't know why. She hated this place. Didn't want anything to do with it." The man let out a scoff. "She even married that cockney wheeler dealer just to annoy our parents. And it worked like a charm! They were furious. And she wondered why she only inherited money instead of the house. It was hardly my fault!"

His loud cry echoed around the room, and he stopped to take a breath.

"I suppose every family has a rebel," Lord Delyn continued. "Ours was no different. Charlie, on the other hand... he was very different from his mother. As he got older, Charlie started taking a keen interest in our side of the family. He used to come and visit whenever he could. Didn't tell his mother, of course. My father was pretty harsh with him. Used to treat him like the family runt. Charlie was always desperate to earn his respect. I'd fallen foul of that game myself and tried to take the boy under my wing, but he wouldn't listen. It was shortly afterwards that he joined the army."

"He joined the army to impress your father?" asked Nesta. "Seems like an extreme measure to take."

Lord Delyn looked up at her and laughed. "You really don't know my family very well, do you?"

He marched over to the doorway and signalled for her to follow. She decided to oblige and made the long walk down a dark hallway until they reached the dining hall.

The lord pointed his cane towards an entire wall of portraits. "There they are," he said. "And that's only a few of the ones who *didn't* die in battle."

Nesta gazed up at the faces of his deceased ancestors. Each one was dressed in a military uniform from a different period in history — everything from The Battle of Waterloo to The Civil War.

"As you can see," said Lord Delyn. "Charlie and myself come from a long line of heroes. The way of the warrior is in our blood."

The way of the moustache also seemed to be hereditary, Nesta thought, looking at the facial hair in each painting. "Charlie must have made his family very proud," she said. "I heard he served in the Falklands."

The elderly man nodded. "I was certainly proud. But that sadly wasn't enough for Charlie." He let out a sigh. "I actually saw him not that long ago. He came to visit me. It had been a while, and something was very different about him. He seemed troubled. As if he were in a very dark place. He kept talking about bravery."

There it was, Nesta thought. That word again — *bravery*. "When you say *dark* place... you don't mean..."

Lord Delyn saw the concern in her face. "Oh, no. I don't mean suicide. But he was definitely hurting. He could be quite obsessive about things. That's something that army life seems to exasperate." He looked back up at the portraits and focused in on his father's stern face. "Many of my ancestors kept journals, you see. They were a way of coping during wartime. Charlie had devoured them all when he was younger, and on his last visit, gave me a copy of his own diary. He was in such a strange mood that day. He placed all of his medals down on this very table and said that they were all meaningless." The man drew his guest's attention to the large dining table. "He told me that he was no hero and to have them all destroyed. He called himself a coward and that my father would have been ashamed. When I tried to ask him what he meant by all of that, he just walked out and left. That was the last time I ever saw him."

Nesta tried to process this new side to the man whose death she had been trying to solve for the past week. It was a far more vulnerable and conflicted side than she had come across so far. "Did you ever read his journal?" she asked.

The lord nodded as though he wished he hadn't. "I was expecting a similar account to all of my other relatives. War and survival hasn't really changed all that much after all these centuries. What I got from Charlie's entries were beyond anything I could have imagined. He wrote of a subject that he had never verbally expressed — certainly not to me, anyway."

His guest waited for him to elaborate but grew impatient. "Well?" Nesta asked. "What was it?"

Lord Delyn stared down at the polished floor and sighed. "He wrote about love."

CHAPTER 23

"Wow," said Darren, as he unloaded another box of knitting.

"Yep," said Nesta, watching him set up their display of bobble hats before shaking her head and rearranging them. She had become quite particular about the layout of her stall, and the teenager didn't seem to possess any care or attention to detail whatsoever.

Darren mulled over everything she had just told him about her recent findings. "You could have waited for me before going to that fancy house. That would have looked great on camera. Every murder mystery case needs a big house with a posh family."

Nesta thought about her visit to Picton Hall during the curious case over at Talacre and suspected that the teenager was probably right. "I feel like we're getting close." She looked around, as Mold market was beginning to come to life for another busy Wednesday. "I'm getting a much clearer picture of Charlie's state of mind before his death. He was experiencing a lot of mental turmoil."

"That's pretty common for war vets," said Darren (whose

knowledge on the subject mainly came from characters that Sylvester Stallone played). He chucked down some baby cardigans which were instantly picked back up and folded. "War does stuff to a person. It can be pretty traumatic."

"So is love and heartbreak," said Nesta, reflecting on what Lord Delyn had told her about the contents of Charlie's journal. She looked up and saw Tony Cockle heading past them with a plant pot in each hand. "Can you hold the fort for a second?" she asked her assistant.

Darren waited for her to disappear and sighed, whilst he opened up another box. "I think I need a raise working here," he muttered.

Tony Cockle was placing the final two flower pots on his stall, when he sensed a person standing there behind him. As a former soldier, he had been trained to possess a keen awareness of his surroundings, and in that moment, his senses were ringing the alarm bells.

"Do you have a minute, Tony?"

The man recognised the voice and grimaced. He hated being disturbed during his morning routine. There were still four more tasks yet to complete before his stall was ready for business, and to hesitate caused him great pain.

After a deep breath, he turned around. "Absolutely. How can I help?"

Nesta smiled. "I've been learning a lot about your old friend, Charlie."

Tony looked surprised. Charlie had not been an easy person to get to know and that was when he was alive. How this woman had managed to find anything out whilst he had been dead was beyond him. "Oh?"

Nesta stepped forward to admire one of his tulips and could feel the man grow tense, as she stroked its petal. "It's amazing how much you can learn about a person from other people," she said. "I suppose that's all we have once we're dead and gone. It doesn't matter what *we* think about ourselves anymore. We no longer exist. We're just a summary of memories in other people's heads. Defined by our actions, and the words that come out of our mouths."

Tony chuckled. "How very philosophical of you. That's pretty heavy stuff for this time on a Wednesday morning. Personally, I couldn't give a monkeys what other people think. Or how they remember me. If I don't care whilst I'm alive, it's unlikely I will when I'm dead and gone."

"Charlie seemed to care a lot about what people thought of him," said Nesta. "Well, certain people, anyway. Like his family."

"How would you know that from what other people told you?" Tony asked with a scoff. "Nobody really knew what Charlie thought except Charlie."

"Exactly." Nesta smiled. "Which is lucky that he wrote it all down in a journal. These were his words and not anybody else's."

Tony nodded. "Yeah, I do remember him keeping a diary. He was always scribbling away in that thing."

"Did he ever speak to you about a love interest of his?" Nesta asked.

"Love?" Tony laughed. "We were soldiers. We'd joke about people we wanted to sleep with or people we *had* slept with. It wasn't the kind of environment to pour our hearts out. Charlie was also my commanding officer. We only really got to know each other more after we left the army. The military creates a brotherly relationship. And brothers don't sit around talking about *love*."

"Strange," said Nesta. "Charlie wrote a lot about the person he was deeply in love with. It sounds like he probably had to if a person couldn't freely talk about it."

Tony didn't seem as convinced. "The guy never married. He

can't have been *that* in love with someone if he never proposed to them."

"This person was different. He wrote about the pain of having to keep this relationship a secret. That he had never loved anyone like that before, and he knew that they felt the same."

"Sounds like he was having an affair with someone who was already married," said Tony.

Nesta nodded. "Yes, I think you're right. He wrote about a person called Lily."

The name caused Tony to go pale. He recognised it immediately, and Nesta could tell.

"You remember a Lily?"

Tony nodded and needed a moment to respond. "He was in my company."

Now it was Nesta's turn to pause. "Lily's a man?"

"Lisle Carmody." Tony cleared his throat. "We served together in the Falklands. We always called him Lily, initially just to annoy him. Then the name stuck. He was older than the rest of us. Him and Charlie were thick as thieves, though. We all noticed it. But I never imagined that they were —" He paused again to take a breath. "The poor guy was killed in action. He never made it back."

Nesta could tell that the news had thrown the man, and she was still processing the added detail of Lily being a fellow soldier. "Where was he from?"

Tony turned to face her. "He was from Mold."

CHAPTER 24

"Well this all just got very complicated," said Darren.

Nesta had returned to the stall with a mind that was still spinning from her conversation with Tony, and she had done her best to fill the teenager in on the most recent development (even if she *was* struggling with it herself).

"It only feels complicated because there's still a missing piece of the puzzle," she said. "Murder is very straightforward in many ways, especially when there's a gun involved. There's a motive, a trigger and someone to pull it. Nothing complicated about that." She was just about to continue, when a hooded figure emerged from the passing crowd. "Look!" she whispered, as a familiar teenager went scurrying past them. "Come on!"

Before he could protest, Darren was pulled along by his arm. "But what about the —"

It seemed that the stall full of knitted goods could look after itself on this occasion, and they ran off in pursuit of an unsuspecting Archie.

The young man maintained a brisk pace and continued his journey down the narrow side streets. Unbeknownst to him, two people were hot on his tail, and they were going to follow him as far as they could without getting detected. A couple of minutes later, and Archie was heading down a long, residential road.

A few houses back, Nesta and Darren had to decrease their speed to a slow dawdle.

"Why are we following him?" asked Darren. "It's not like he's going to tell us anything."

"Because I want to find out where he lives," Nesta snapped. Her question was soon to be answered, as the young man up ahead turned into a front garden. "Stop!"

The two followers froze in front of a bus stop, and Nesta jumped into a more casual position by leaning against a wall.

Darren was shoved into a similar posture that was very much against his will. "What are you doing?"

"Just act natural!"

The teenager looked around at the empty street. "How is anything that we're doing natural?"

Nesta ignored him and focused on her target. Archie had disappeared into a modest bungalow and was now safely out of view.

"Now we wait," Nesta said.

"For what?" Darren asked.

"What do you think? We wait for that young man to come back outside."

Darren groaned. "I'm not waiting here all morning. We'll confuse the buses. I might as well hop on one whilst I'm at it. I've done enough steak-outs for one summer holiday."

Despite his complaining, which lasted several more minutes, the two spies did not have to wait long. Archie burst back outside through the front door of his house in a fit of blind rage. A woman's voice called out to him from inside the bungalow but it failed to deter his determined strides.

"Here he comes," said Nesta. "This is our chance to corner him."

Darren began to look worried. "Are you nuts? The guy's supposedly got a gun!"

"Quiet! Or he'll hear us!"

Archie marched back up the street like a man on a mission. He had the face of someone who had just been through a domestic argument and appeared hell bent on getting as far away from his house as possible. Unfortunately for him, a woman seemed to appear out of nowhere to block his path.

"Hello, Archie."

Nesta had stepped out in front of him and was staring him down like a teacher in a detention hall.

Archie looked over to see Darren standing nearby and couldn't help but take a few steps back. "What do you two want?" he asked.

Nesta crossed her arms and smiled. "I think we need a little talk."

The confused teenager couldn't help but laugh off her suggestion. "Get out of my way, you weirdos!" He swerved around her and began walking back towards the centre of town.

"Maybe I should speak to your parents instead!" Nesta called after him. Her threat was enough to make him stop. "Do they know about the gun?"

Archie came marching back with a concerned face. "I don't know what you're talking about!"

"No?" Nesta squared up to him, until he began leaning his back against the brick wall. "Then maybe I should try the police. I'm sure they would be interested."

"Are you blackmailing me?" asked Archie. His voice had gone up a few octaves, as his hands began to tremble.

"Call it what you like," said Nesta. "But you're going to tell me everything I need to know about how you came across that gun. And I mean *everything*."

Archie swallowed an enormous gulp and prepared to share a story that had been plaguing his mind for days. Whether he knew it himself or not, this was something he really needed to get off his chest.

CHAPTER 25

The Welsh flag was flying high on the tower of St Mary's Church when Nesta approached. She had walked away from the busy market to experience a much quieter end of the street and was pleased to discover that she wasn't the only one.

Dorothy was in her usual spot at this time of the day, sitting on the wooden bench with her back facing the church wall.

"I thought I might find you here," said Nesta, taking a seat beside her.

The woman chuckled. "I'm as predictable as that clock," she said and pointed to the church behind them. "I always need a break from all those people on market day. It gets a bit much after a while."

"I know the feeling."

They sat in silence for a moment, listening to the gentle birdsong.

"I never knew your last name was Carmody," Nesta said, eventually.

Dorothy barely flinched at the mention of her surname. "Everyone calls me Dorothy. How did you know that?"

"I didn't for sure. But I had a strong feeling."

Dorothy turned to look at her. "You are a funny one. People think I'm funny. Maybe you're psychic."

Nesta nodded. "I wish I was. It would have made getting to the bottom of all this carry on a lot easier." The woman beside her remained quiet. "I'm sorry to hear about your husband. I know what it feels like to lose someone."

Dorothy's smile vanished and a seriousness washed over her face. "It was a very long time ago."

"Yes, but if there's anything I know about grief, it's that it never truly goes away. Not when you love someone. There are certain memories that never leave us."

"You're right there," said Dorothy. "My memory seems to be very selective at times."

"So I've realised." She let out a deep breath. "You never told me about seeing Archie that day." Nesta continued to look straight ahead towards a row of shops on the other side of the street but could feel the woman's curious gaze on her. "He told me that he found you holding an old pistol. You were sitting right here when he walked past with his two friends." Dorothy continued to stare but said nothing. "Archie mentioned that there was a silencer attached, which the groundsman later found in the grass. They didn't believe it was real, and you gave it to them so they could find out."

"They're a naughty little bunch," said Dorothy. Her voice was dry and croaky. "I had no further use for it. If that little Archie wanted to prove himself and be a big man, he was welcome to it."

"You honestly gave a loaded weapon to a group of teenagers?" asked Nesta, who had hoped it wasn't true.

"Those kids have had it coming a long time." Dorothy's face had darkened at the mere thought of them. "They go around tormenting this entire town and get away with it. The residents of Mold are good, honest people. Someone needed to teach those boys a lesson. With any luck, the police will give them the punishment that they deserve."

"By handing them a murder weapon? Was that the plan all along?"

Dorothy laughed and shook her head. "My dear, you really have no idea. Archie and his friends were just at the right place at the right time."

"I know they were responsible for the gunshot I heard. They ran around the church and fired it into a gravestone. But they weren't responsible for killing Charlie." Dorothy remained quiet as though she was boring her. "I also know that Charlie was in a relationship with your late husband. Did you know that?"

Dorothy snapped her head around to glare at her. "Of course I know!" she hissed. "I discovered years ago that my Lisle was a cheat. I'm not stupid. I found a whole box of letters when I was clearing out the attic. Although, I didn't know that his secret lover was a fellow soldier. The letters were all signed with the letter C." Her eyes burned with rage. "Do you know how hard it is to find out that your war-hero husband was a lying cheat? I had to live with that for decades."

"When did you find out that it was Charlie?" asked Nesta.

"Last week. When Charlie asked me to meet him in the church graveyard." Dorothy cleared her throat. "I'd got to know him quite well since he moved to Mold. He seemed like a nice enough man. I found him standing at the grave of one of his ancestors. He was in a strange mood and started telling me some heroic war story that he'd read about. Then he went on to describe the day my husband died." She pulled out a tissue and wiped her eye. "Lisle went down with the RFA Sir Galahad that was bombed during the Falklands war. Charlie was on that ship, too. He told me that he'd visited Lisle's cabin on the morning that they were hit. The same morning Lisle decided to end their relationship."

Nesta thought about the love that Charlie supposedly had for this man. She was also aware of the destruction of a broken heart. "I take it that didn't go down too well."

"Charlie said he pleaded with him," Dorothy continued. "He begged him not to end it, until Lisle struck him in the face. That was around the time that their ship came under heavy fire. My husband was so badly wounded that he could barely walk when the ship began to sink. Charlie said that he watched him beg for his help. But, instead of helping, he left his own fellow soldier behind to drown." Nesta listened to every word with a heavy heart. She hated the thought of anyone pleading for their life. "He told me that he'd lived with that decision his entire life. That it had haunted him every day. He called himself a coward and handed me an old hand gun. He said it was only right that I got my revenge for the death of my husband. That he craved a soldier's death. Charlie moved close enough so that I couldn't miss." Dorothy's eyes watered, as she relived the moment of her finger quivering against the trigger. "I said he was no soldier. And it wasn't my husband's death that I wanted to avenge. I wanted justice for having the memories of my entire marriage shredded to pieces — for making me feel betrayed for all those years. Happy memories are all we have to hold onto in the end. And that man robbed me of every single one. I could have lived with having a husband that died in battle. But one who cheated on our entire marriage?" A tear streamed down her cheek. "I was more than happy to pull the trigger."

Both women went silent and listened to the bells of St Mary's Church.

Nesta was reminded of Ernest Hemingway's famous novel and that the title had a whole new meaning during that quiet moment. She stood up and turned around to face the clock tower. The church, as it always did, seemed so peaceful. Without saying another word, she left the local woman on her bench and headed back towards the market.

CHAPTER 26

"Taylor! Kim! Get down from there!"

The two cockapoos ignored Nesta's cries and continued to dig their teeth into the bed sheet pinned up against the bedroom wall.

"Was that thing really necessary?" she asked after finishing her last take.

"It bounces the light and creates an even tone," said Darren, lowering his phone to stop the video recording. The white sheet flopped down to the ground and was pounced on by two determined dogs. Hari sat on the bed, watching the entire scene with sheer disapproval.

"How was it?" Nesta asked. She headed over to look over his shoulder at the latest video for his true crime channel.

"It's not bad," Darren muttered. "But maybe we should have done it away from the window.

"I don't mean how it *looks*! I'm talking about the content of what I'm saying." She began pacing the room and lifted up her arms like a thespian ruminating on her performance. "I felt like it really wrapped everything up nicely. Especially with the themes of war and death."

A bemused Darren stared at her. "Yeah, sure. Why not?"

Nesta sighed and checked her watch. "Oh! They'll be ready now."

She headed downstairs to the smell of freshly-baked biscuits, only to be interrupted by the doorbell.

"I'm coming!" she cried. After chucking the hot tray against the stove, Nesta scurried to the front door and swung it open.

"We're back!" Erin stood on her own doorstep with bronzed skin and an excited face. She grabbed her mother and squeezed her tight. Her boyfriend, Duncan, stood beside her with his enormous forearms that bulged out of his tight t-shirt.

"How are my babies?" Erin asked, as they headed inside. "Have they been behaving?"

"Oh, they've been as good as gold," Nesta muttered.

"There they are! Come here, my cutie puties!"

Taylor and Kim came running down the stairs to greet their doting owner.

After getting over the shock of seeing her damaged sofa, Erin went on to fill her mother in on every detail of their hotel, whilst Nesta brought out a tray of biscuits.

"How was the baking course?"

"Invaluable," said Nesta. "Maybe the proof's in the pudding. How about you try one of these."

The young couple bit into her biscuits and pulled similar disgusted faces.

"Get up to anything else exciting whilst we were away?" asked Duncan with a smug grin.

Nesta paused to think. "Not really. It was a pretty quiet week apart from the murder case."

Erin and Duncan both let out a hysterical laugh and Nesta was forced to join them.

"That's a good one Mrs G," said Duncan. "Mold's full of brutal homicides. Like Hell's Kitchen in Wales."

"More like Hell's Cupboard," said Erin.

They were about to laugh again, when Darren came running down the stairs. "Did you want me to put the bed back together?" he asked.

Erin and Duncan both looked at each other.

"Oh," said Nesta. "How rude of me. This is my friend Darren."

The teenager gave the couple an awkward wave.

"Sorry," said Erin, trying to clear her throat. "Did you just say that this young man was your friend?"

Nesta gave her an innocent nod and placed a hand on Darren's shoulder. "Why, yes. We've been busy filming some videos up in your bedroom. I hope you don't mind."

Duncan almost choked on a mouthful of biscuit. "Hey," he said to his girlfriend. "Why don't you give your mam her present?"

"Oh, yes!" Erin was happy to change the subject and went running over to her bags.

Nesta was soon handed an envelope. "What's this for?"

"Just another little something to say thank you," said Erin. She watched her pull out a large gift certificate with a large heading: *The Legion Hotel*. "It's an entire week away at one of Chester's finest hotels!"

Her mother was lost for words. She had always liked Chester, but the idea of staying in a posh hotel was rather daunting. "You really shouldn't have."

"You deserve it, mam! It's a chance to spoil yourself a little." Erin turned to her boyfriend. "Duncan's brother knows someone who works there and got us a huge discount, didn't he, love?"

"He sure did," said Duncan. "Don't look so terrified, Nesta! There won't be any murders at *this* hotel!"

Nesta and Darren looked at each other, whilst the couple before them howled with laughter.

"Well," said Nesta, gazing down at the hotel name again. "Fingers crossed, then. I guess you never know when you might get lucky."

ABOUT THE AUTHOR

We hope you enjoyed this book. Reviews are extremely important for new authors, so please do feel free to write a short review on the book's Amazon page.

Whilst you're waiting for Book 4 in this new series, why not try the first book in another P. L Handley murder mystery series:

The Murder Ledger
By P. L. Handley
Available on Amazon

If you'd like to read more books in this new series, you can join the P. L. Handley e-mail newsletter and receive all the latest news on future releases.

Subscribe to the e-mailing list by visiting the official P. L. Handley website at: www.plhandley.com

THE MURDER LEDGER

When an elderly lottery winner goes missing in a small, rural town, it's up to a tenacious, local reporter to solve the case. Aided by a curious accountant with a methodical brain, Rhiannon must use her new (and unlikely) partnership to uncover a series of shocking secrets.

Printed in Dunstable, United Kingdom